"Give me the baby. . . ."

I began backing toward the hall. Before I had gone three feet, the closet door burst open.

I started to scream. That may not sound real brave and manly, but tell me what *you* would do if your closet door blew open and you saw a green-skinned, red-eyed, fang-mouthed monster inside; a monster bathed in green light and surrounded by billows of curling smoke; a monster who raised one enormous muscle-bound arm, pointed it right at you, and said, "Give me the baby. . . ."

Look for future Bruce Coville titles from Scholastic:

Bruce Coville's Book of Aliens
Bruce Coville's Book of Ghosts
Bruce Coville's Book of Nightmares

BRUCE COVILLE'S
BOOK OF

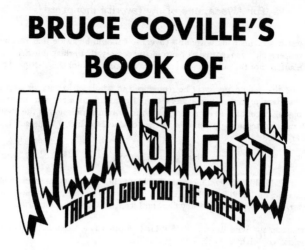

Compiled and edited by
Bruce Coville

Illustrated by
John Pierard

A GLC Book

AN
APPLE
PAPERBACK

SCHOLASTIC INC.
New York Toronto London Auckland Sydney

For Alyssa, one of my favorite monsters

ISBN 0-590-46159-1

10 9 8 7 6 5 4 3 2   3 4 5 6 7 8/9

Printed in the U.S.A.   40

First Scholastic printing, September 1993

CONTENTS

INTRODUCTION:
WELCOME TO THE WILD RUMPUS

So you love monsters, huh? Well, you've come to the right place. You are about to enter a monster-filled collection of thirteen stories (okay, twelve stories and a poem) that will make you laugh and make you shiver—sometimes both at once.

Actually, this is the first of four collections of stories I am preparing for kids who like the same kind of weird and spooky things that I do. Each book will focus on one of my favorite subjects—starting with monsters and moving on to aliens, then ghosts, and ending up with pure fear! I'll provide the opening story for each book, then share with you a variety of stories from other authors, stories I think you will really enjoy. (I may even sneak in one or two more of my own along the way, as I've done in this book.)

Some of these stories will be ones I have found by searching through stacks of books for the

kind of tale I know my readers like; most, however, will be brand new—commissioned just for
these collections. That's one of the best parts of
doing a book like this, by the way: It gives me
a chance to call other writers and say, "Hey,
how would you like to write a monster story for
me?"

I'm glad we're starting with monsters. I've
had a special place in my heart for them ever since
I was a kid myself. (It's a little room marked "For
Monsters Only.")

My first experience with monster stories, at
least the first I remember, happened with a babysitter. She was the kind of babysitter every kid
wants—the kind who can scare you to death! She
had just been to a re-release of the original Boris
Karloff *Frankenstein,* and while my little brother
and I sat with wide eyes, she told us the whole
story. It would be several years before I saw the
film myself, but my babysitter had recounted it in
such vivid detail that I felt as if I had seen it that
night.

It was terrifying, *and I loved every minute of
it.* That was it: I was hooked on monsters for
life.

That should give you part of the answer to
one of the most common questions I get from
kids: "Why do you write about monsters so
often?"

Another part of the answer is that I write

about monsters because kids like to read about them.

But why is *that* true?

I think one reason is that most of us have times when we want to be *like* monsters. I mean, think about it: Monsters are big and strong, and when they get angry, they don't have to hold it in and try to act polite. They can just roar around scaring the daylights out of everyone!

Also, monsters and kids have a lot in common. After all, these strange and terrifying creatures (I mean monsters, not kids) are often feared, misunderstood, and picked on. Not only that, they're usually judged by their looks, rather than by who they really are. Or by their reputations. Happens to kids all the time.

In the stories that follow you will find monsters who are terrible, and monsters with hearts of gold; monsters who will make you laugh—or scare you silly; a veritable jamboree of monsters of every shape and size, waiting just for you.

So read on. Or, as it says in the pages of one of the greatest monster stories of all time: "Let the wild rumpus start!"

P.S. In case you don't remember where "Let the wild rumpus start!" comes from, I'll give you a clue: The character who said it was named Max. If you still don't remember, look on page 164, and I'll tell you the name of the story in which he said it.

P.P.S. Look in the back of the book for an exciting announcement.

I bet everyone who has a little brother has called the kid a monster at some time or other. When I started wondering what would happen if that was really true, out came this story.

MY LITTLE BROTHER IS A MONSTER

Bruce Coville

I. Basket Case

Thump!

We both heard it, even above the late-March wind that was whipping around the house. Mom looked up from the strand of red yarn she was weaving through the warp of her big loom and said, "Go see what that was, would you, Jason?"

I sighed, but it was mostly for effect. Despite the open math book in front of me, I was doing more daydreaming than figuring. So it made sense for me to go, rather than for Mom to interrupt her work.

However, what I saw when I opened the front

door convinced me she should be interrupted after all. "Mom!" I yelled over the wind. "You'd better come here. *Now!*"

She reached the front hall in time to see me carry in the big black basket. After the last few years she's gotten pretty good at taking whatever comes along right in stride, so when she saw the baby inside, she didn't wig out. She just said, "Oh, the poor little fellow."

"What makes you think it's a boy?"

"Mothers know these things," she replied, reaching down to chuck the baby under the chin.

While Mom fussed over the baby, I took another look at the basket. It was woven from thick, dark twigs. After a moment I spotted a piece of coarse paper tucked next to the baby. When I pulled it out and unfolded it, I found this note:

> Tu Whoom I Mae Consarn,
> Pleeze tayk carr of mie babie. I cannut doo it, and I want mie litul dum pling tu hav a gud home. Thiss is moor importun than yew kan gess.
>
> Tank yew veree muck

It was signed with an X.

"Better take a look at this," I said.

Mom read the note, wiped away a tear, and picked up the baby. "I'm so sorry, Little Dumpling. But I'm glad your mother brought you here. We'll take care of you."

Little Dumpling puked on her shoulder.

"How do you know the note came from its mother?" I asked as I went to fetch the paper towels. "Couldn't it have been the father?"

"Mothers know these things."

I was getting a little sick of that line; Mom had been using it a lot since she and Dad divorced three years ago.

Probably I should have seen it coming when we kept the baby with us that night. But we live way out in the country, so it made sense when Mom said it was too late to take him anywhere else.

I did get suspicious when she managed to get too busy to contact the authorities the next day.

By the third day I was certain: She wasn't planning on doing anything about the baby anytime soon.

To tell you the truth, I wasn't sure I wanted her to; I was starting to like the little guy myself. On the other hand, I was worried that we might get into trouble.

"Don't we have to go to the police?" I asked that night as we were hauling my old crib up from the basement.

Mom shook her head. "I've been thinking about it, and the fact is the police will just take him to a foster home. But Little Dumpling's mother chose *us* to take care of him. So that's what we're going to do. Besides, it will be good for you to have a baby brother, and the way things look now, this is the only one you're likely to get."

Then she tried to tell me that sharing my room with him was a treat. What kind of a "treat" it really was I discovered two weeks later, on the night of the full moon.

I had gone to bed early, mostly because I had joined the baseball team, and we were practicing so hard that my body felt like someone had put me inside a giant can and given me a good shaking.

Little Dumpling was already sacked out in my old crib.

(Yes, we were still calling him Little Dumpling—L.D. for short. I think that was because naming him would have made it seem like he really was ours, and Mom was still half expecting the real mother to show up and want him back.)

I peeked in the crib. L.D.'s eyes were scrinched shut, and he was clutching the green plastic rattle I had bought him out of my allowance. (All right, so I'm a sucker; babies do that kind of thing to people.)

"G'night, Bonzo," I whispered.

"Bonzo" was my private name for him. I got

4

it from an old movie I saw on TV one night, something costarring Ronald Reagan and a chimpanzee (Bonzo was the chimp).

After climbing into bed, I turned out the light on my nightstand. I listened to the soft rain pattering against my window and the April wind rustling through the new leaves on the oaks and maples that surround the old house we had moved to after Dad left. I was asleep in seconds.

When I woke the moon was shining through the window, and Little Dumpling was making a weird noise. I got out of bed to see if he was all right.

When I looked in the crib, I nearly wet my pants.

The baby was covered with fur!

He opened his eyes and smiled at me.

Fangs!

I began backing toward the door. "Mom?" I called nervously.

My voice didn't seem to be working. I tried again. This time it worked better than I expected: "MOM! GET IN HERE!"

In seconds she was pounding through my door, pulling on her robe as she ran. "What is it, Jason? Did something happen to the baby?"

Ignoring the fact that it would have been nice if she had asked if *I* was all right, I gasped. "T-t-t-take a look at him!"

She ran to the crib. "What is it?" she asked again.

"What do you mean, 'What is it?' He's covered with fur!"

She looked at me as if I had lost my mind. "Jason, are *you* all right?"

Now she asks.

"Of course *I'm* all right. Little Dumpling's the one who just turned into a monster!"

"Jason, come here," she said in that quiet-but-firm voice that signals she means business. Nervously I joined her at the crib. L.D. was sleeping soundly, sucking his thumb and looking cute as the dickens. The only hair I could see was the brownish black fuzz that covered his adorable little head.

I rubbed my eyes. "But . . . but . . ."

"You had a bad dream, sweetheart."

I shook my head. "I *wasn't* dreaming. It was real. He was covered with fur. And he had *fangs.*"

Even as I said it, I realized how stupid I sounded. For a moment I wondered if I *had* been dreaming. But it really had happened. I was as sure of that as I was that there was no way I could convince my mother of what I had seen.

"Try to get back to sleep, honey," Mom said. "You'll feel better in the morning."

I considered arguing, but what would happen? She would be convinced I was nuts—might even insist I see a shrink. And then what? If I tried to convince a doctor that my baby brother was a

6

monster, I might end up locked in a rubber room until they could "cure my delusions," as they say in the movies.

I climbed back into bed. But I didn't turn out my light.

I had no intention of going back to sleep.

II. Something in a Closet

In the end, sleep won. When I woke the next morning, I had a moment when I wondered if I actually had been dreaming. No; it had happened. The only thing I *couldn't* believe was that I had fallen back asleep afterward.

I sighed. If I had known I was going to fall asleep anyway, I would have tried to do it earlier. I was exhausted.

Little Dumpling started making "pick me up" noises. We had gotten into a routine by that time: When I woke up each morning I would haul him out of the crib and take him to the kitchen, where Mom would be making breakfast. Then I would feed him. I got a kick out it, because he was so sloppy when he ate and liked to smear oatmeal all over himself.

I wasn't sure what to expect when I went to the edge of the crib that morning. But Little Dumpling was holding out his chubby arms and looking like his regular self.

"Up!" he commanded in a cute baby voice.

I blinked. "When did *you* learn to talk?" I asked.

He smiled, showing a tooth. It was short and square—a baby tooth, not a fang. But baby teeth don't come in overnight, at least not according to my father, who used to love to tell how miserable I had made him while cutting *my* first tooth.

Maybe *this* would convince my mother something weird was going on. But did I actually want to carry this kid into the kitchen? What if that cute little tooth turned into a fang once I got him close to my neck?

"UP!" he repeated urgently.

"Jason!" called my mother. "Time for breakfast. Bring the baby into the kitchen, would you, honey?"

I sighed. "Come on, Bonzo," I said, reaching down to lift him. He snuggled against me, and I felt my heart melt.

Babies are dangerous that way.

"He talked this morning," I said as Mom fastened L.D. into his high chair. (Actually, it was *my* high chair, from when I was a baby. I didn't want it, of course. Even so, it felt weird to have this kid using all my old stuff.)

"Don't be silly, Jason," said Mom as she tied a bib around his neck. "He can't be more than six months old. Babies don't talk at that age."

"And he grew a tooth," I added, knowing that at least I could prove that much.

"Are you serious?" Before I could stop her, she poked a finger into L.D.'s mouth and ran it over his gums. I was terrified. If he bit her, would *she* turn into a monster? But after a second she turned to me and said, "What has gotten into you, Jason? There's no tooth here."

"But I saw it!"

"Jason . . ."

"Let me try," I said, sticking my finger into L.D.'s mouth.

He gummed me pretty hard. But there was no tooth to be found. I pulled my finger out in disgust.

L.D. smiled at me—a big, happy baby smile.

"Goo," he said, blowing a spit bubble.

It was cute. But it didn't melt my heart.

It sent cold shivers down my spine.

Tired and worried, I had a hard time concentrating in school that day. And I totally screwed up baseball practice because my mind was on the baby instead of the ball. I wondered if Mom was safe, home alone with that little monster. But nothing happened that day (or night)—or the next —or the next. After several nearly sleepless nights, I began to wonder if I had dreamed it after all.

Or maybe nothing was going to happen until the night of the next full moon. . . .

That was it—it had to be! It was the moon

that brought out the monster in our little found-
ling.

Of course, I thought, *just being a monster
doesn't necessarily mean that he's a menace.*

You can probably see what the problem was.
The longer we had him, the more I was getting to
like him. All right, all right, I guess I even sort of
loved him. I'm only saying that because I'm trying
to tell you everything, straight out. It's not something I would admit if I didn't have to, but it ties
into the way things worked out.

Anyway, I decided that next full moon I
would sneak the video camera into my bedroom
and tape a record of just what happened to Little
Dumpling during the night.

Of course, that meant staying in the bedroom
myself. I had planned to avoid that, but I figured
better to get this over with as soon as possible. For
one thing, Little Dumpling was growing pretty
fast. Not fast enough to be wildly abnormal, but
fast enough that even Mom had commented on it.

I wanted to settle this before he got *too*
big.

It was a weird month. About halfway through
it, something began howling in the distance at
night. Mom claimed it was a neighbor's dog. I
wasn't so certain.

Even worse were the noises that started coming from my closet at night. I tried to tell Mom

about them, but again, I could see that she thought I was crazy. I started checking the door every morning, to see if there were claw marks on the back of it or anything. I was never sure whether I wanted to find them or not. It would be proof that something weird was going on. But what would it mean if I *did* find them?

I wished Dad were still with us. I did call him a couple of times, but I found I wasn't able to tell him what was going on. He was nice, but I didn't feel connected to him, didn't feel as if he could help me, save me, from what was happening.

By the time the next full moon came, I was a nervous wreck.

Things might have gone differently that night if Mom hadn't been asked out on a date. Usually I don't mind when she goes out, though I would rather she was seeing my father, trying to get things back together. But this time I did mind. When she asked me to keep an eye on Little Dumpling, I panicked.

"You can't go out tonight!" I cried. "It's the full moon."

Mom got mad, which doesn't happen often. "Any more nonsense like that, Jason Burger, and you can forget watching *Creature Feature* until you're forty. This is a special evening; Delbert got these tickets weeks ago. And L.D. will be asleep before we leave. I just want you here in case of emergency. You've got a whole list of people to call if anything actually comes up."

Right. Like Mrs. Ferguson down the road would be any help if L.D. actually turned into a fur-bearing fang-beast!

Well, at least there wouldn't be anyone around to hassle me about using the video camera. . . .

Under the circumstances, I didn't think it would be possible to fall asleep—which was why I was so astonished to find myself waking up some time later.

The full moon was shining through my window.

I blinked, trying to remember what I was supposed to be doing. The snorts coming from L.D.'s crib brought everything back to me. It was monster time!

I grabbed the camera and stood on the end of the bed, hoping the moon would provide enough light to show the transformation. Silently, for fear a sound might stop whatever was going on, I focused on Little Dumpling.

My mouth went dry. Even though he was still asleep, fur was sprouting all over his body—at least the parts of it that I could see. His ears were getting pointy. Even worse, he had to be a half foot taller than when we had put him to bed!

I pressed the trigger on the camera. The slight whir woke Little Dumpling. He opened his eyes, blinked, then scrambled to his feet—a kid-size monster in yellow ducky pajamas that were splitting at the seams. Grabbing the bars on the side of the crib, he began to shake them. Then he threw back his head and howled. A cold shiver spasmed down my spine. It was time to get out of there.

Before I could move, I was distracted by another set of noises. These came not from the crib but from the closet. Turning, I saw a sliver of light under the door. That was scary enough, given the fact that *my closet didn't have a light in it.* But when green smoke started curling under the door, I thought my heart was going to stop.

Before I could decide whether to run for it or stay and try to protect Little Dumpling, I heard something scratching at the *window*!

What was going on around here?

"Up!" pleaded a low voice. "Up! Up!"

It was L.D., standing in his crib and holding out his furry arms. I hesitated, then grabbed him, hoping he wouldn't sink his fangs into my neck.

"We have to get out of here, Bonzo," I said as the closet door started to rattle.

"Out!" he agreed happily.

I began backing toward the hall. Before I had gone three feet, the closet door burst open.

III. Mazrak and Keegel Farzym

I started to scream. That may not sound real brave and manly, but tell me what *you* would do if your closet door blew open and you saw a green-skinned, red-eyed, fang-mouthed monster inside; a monster bathed in green light and surrounded by billows of curling smoke; a monster who raised one enormous, muscle-bound arm, pointed it right at you, and said, "Give me that baby," in a voice that sounded like rocks being smashed together.

"NO!" cried Little Dumpling, throwing his arms around my neck. "NO NO NO!"

Now he decided to be frightened. For an instant I had hoped he might yell, "Daddy!" Then I could have let the two of them work things out while I got my butt out of there.

Actually, I would have gotten my butt out of there at that point anyway, if not for three things:

(1) My legs seemed to have stopped working.

(2) The monster didn't seem to be able to move out of the closet; it was straining forward, as if pushing at some invisible barrier.

(3) The *window* blew open, and a blue monster with a long gray beard leaned through and growled, "If you want to live to see morning, follow me!"

I knew I wanted to live to see morning. I

didn't know if following this guy was the best way to do that. Little Dumpling was no help; furry face buried against my shoulder, he was whimpering, "No, no! Bad, bad, bad!" But whether he was referring to the first monster, the second monster, or life in general, I had no way of telling.

The monster in the closet turned to the monster in the window and growled, "Do not interfere, Keegel Farzym!" Then he turned back to me and bellowed, "Give . . . me . . . that . . . child!" At the same time he thrust his right arm into the room. The tearing sound that accompanied this action made me think he had actually ripped through the invisible force. His hand—enormous and green, with long fingers that ended in black, razor-sharp claws—stretched toward me.

When I turned to run, my bedroom door slammed shut.

I grabbed the knob, turned, pulled. It wouldn't budge.

"No, no!" whimpered Little Dumpling, tightening his grip on my neck. "Bad, bad, *bad!*"

Another shredding sound. I turned. The closet-monster had managed to thrust its other arm into the room. Now it was leaning forward, stretching both arms toward us.

"Mazrak will break through in seconds!" cried the monster at the window. "If you don't want to die, come here *now!*"

The door still wouldn't budge. Mazrak was getting louder. Suddenly the window didn't seem like such a bad idea except heading for it meant I had to pass uncomfortably close to the closet. Mazrak roared and lunged for me as I passed, but what was left of the invisible barrier held.

"Give me the baby," said Keegel Farzym.

I hesitated, until Little Dumpling turned and reached toward him. I decided to trust the kid's instincts—I figured he would know more about monsters than I did—and handed him over. The blue monster tucked Little Dumpling under his right arm. Holding the sill with his left hand, he swung sideways. "Climb onto my back!" he growled.

Another roar from the closet. More ripping. A claw brushed against my neck. Yelping with fear, I scrambled onto Keegel Farzym's back.

He jumped.

As we hit the ground, I heard a ferocious roar. Looking over my shoulder, I saw Mazrak's face in the window.

"Run!" I screamed. "He's coming!"

My shout was hardly necessary; Keegel Farzym was already barreling along at a good clip. But he was handicapped by the fact that he was carrying Little Dumpling in front of him and had me clinging to his back. So when I saw Mazrak squeeze through the window and jump to the

ground, I feared it wouldn't be long before he caught up with us.

I had an urge to kick Keegel Farzym in the side and shout "Giddyup!" But I didn't know if that would encourage him to run faster or simply to turn around and kill me. I sank my fingers into his beard—the hairs were thick as my mother's yarn—and held on for dear life.

Soon I saw where we were heading: the cemetery.

Moments later we raced through the iron gate. The full moon caused the shadows of the tombstones to stretch ahead of us like open graves. Mazrak was only steps behind us. The sound of his voice was terrifying—though not as terrifying as knowing that if he caught up with us, I would be the first thing he reached. I braced myself for the first swipe of his claws. But the gate, which had been rusted open for as long as I could remember, slammed shut behind us. I had a feeling Keegel Farzym did it, though I wasn't sure how.

Mazrak grabbed the iron bars. Howling with rage, he shook them until they burst open again. But Keegel Farzym's tactic had bought us enough time to reach one of the mausoleums—the little buildings that stood on some of the family plots.

I was afraid we would be trapped if we went inside. But when we shot through the door, I saw no walls, only a thick, gray mist woven through

with strands of blue light. Keegel Farzym continued to run. It should have taken no more than a
second to cross the floor. I braced myself, expecting to slam into the far wall.

Ten seconds later we were still running, the
mist was getting thicker, and I heard a waterfall
off to our left.

"Where are we going?" I cried.

"To the Land of Always October," panted
Keegel Farzym.

IV. *The Woven Worlds*

Several minutes after we had left the mist, we
entered a boggy, foresty place that looked like
something out of the movies I get to watch on
Saturday nights when my mother is in a good
mood. We stopped underneath a large tree.

"I think we've lost him," panted Keegel
Farzym. "With any luck he won't have been able
to enter that mausoleum, which will mean he'll
have to go back through your closet to get home."

That was good news. If Mazrak was going
home, wherever that was, it meant he wouldn't be
waiting around to get my mother when she came
back from her date. I had started to worry about
that.

"Get down, would you please?" said the monster, squatting so that I could get off his back

without having to jump. Once down, I leaned against the tree and looked around. Swampy forest stretched as far as I could see. Mist curled among the trees. A wolf—or something—howled in the distance.

I decided that I wanted to go home myself. I wondered what the odds of that were.

"Are you going to kill us?" I asked.

Keegel Farzym laughed. It sounded like someone dropping rocks on a kettle drum. "If I had wanted you to die, I would have left you in your room."

That made sense.

I reached up for L.D. Keegel Farzym, who was about twice my height, handed the furry little monster down to me.

"Why did you bring us here?" I asked.

"Did you have someplace safer in mind?"

I thought of Mazrak and shivered. "Not really. But what's going on? Who are you? Why did you save us? *Did* you save us? Why was that other monster after us? What is this all about, anyway?"

He laughed at my barrage of questions. Then a serious look crossed his face. He ran a gnarled blue hand through his long gray beard. His broad nostrils flared, and he stuck out his jaw, causing his lower fangs to sparkle in the moonlight. "I am Keegel Farzym," he said at last, extending a blue hand.

I hesitated, then put out my own hand for him to shake. "My name is Jason. Pleased to meet you—I guess. I mean, *am* I pleased to meet you?"

All right, I was blithering. But it was the first time I ever talked to someone who was nine feet tall and blue. And I still didn't know whether he was on our side or simply an enemy of the other monster that had been after us.

"Most monsters would consider meeting me a great honor."

"Why?"

"I am the High Poet of Always October. I am also guardian of Dum Pling, who is a very important child."

"He is?" I asked in surprise. Then I narrowed my eyes and added, "How did you know we called him Little Dumpling?"

It was Keegel Farzym's turn to look surprised. "Dum Pling is his name," he said, making it two words, like a first name and a last name.

"You name your kids things like Dumb?" I asked in disgust.

"In the secret language of monsters, the word *Bob* means 'the sound of a large dog puking.' However, that does not make us think that when your people name someone Bob that that is what they are calling him. Here the word *Dum* means 'Prince.' The baby's name, translated into your language, would be something along the lines of 'Prince Albert.' "

I glanced at Little Dumpling. He was squishing mud between his toes and eating a bug.

"Are you telling me this little monster is a *prince?*"

"If he lives, he will one day be king of the Land of Always October," rumbled Keegel Farzym, waving a huge, hairy arm around him.

I followed his gesture with my eyes. Until now I had been too distracted to notice that the trees were glowing with all the colors of autumn. I shifted uneasily. Dead leaves rustled beneath my feet. The smell of fall was thick in the air.

I shivered. It had been May when we entered the cemetery.

"This is the Land of Always October," said Keegel Farzym, "where twilight lasts for half a day, the moon is always full, and the sun is rarely seen. This is the home of the folk that you call monsters; the place that haunts your dreams at night, when you remember something frightening yet wonderful; the place you fear, yet cannot stand to stay away from."

Little Dumpling looked up at the huge monster. A smile creased his furry little face.

I was still confused. "If Little Dumpling is the prince of the monsters, how did he end up sleeping in my old crib?"

"Ah," said Keegel Farzym. "Therein lies our problem. Come, we have a long way to go before we reach our destination. Walk with me, and I

will speak to you of many things, of woven worlds, and infant kings."

Despite this promise, we traveled without speaking for several minutes. Keegel Farzym carried Little Dumpling. I walked beside them, except when I had to drop back because the path grew too narrow. The full moon shimmered on the murky water and silvered the mist that twisted through the gnarled trunks of the great trees.

Weird cries echoed in the distance.

Twice we crossed paths that twisted into the darkness, looking both scary and irresistible.

We walked beneath a cliff. At the top loomed a mansion. A single light shone in its tower window.

"Who lives up there?" I asked.

"It depends," replied Keegel Farzym with a shrug.

It was the first question I had asked since we began walking. I had been waiting for him to start his story, but for some reason he seemed reluctant.

After another several minutes curiosity overcame caution, and I said, "Are you going to tell me what's going on?"

A bat flew overhead. Keegel Farzym, his hand moving faster than I could see, snatched it from the air and popped it into his mouth. He chewed for a minute, then spit out a bone, all the while staring into the distance. Finally he turned to me and said, "The Land of Always October is in danger."

"I'm sorry to hear that," I said sincerely. "But what does that have to do with me?"

"A great deal, if my theory is correct. With you, and every other human in your world. Not in the sense that it is your fault, but in the sense that you are in danger, too."

"What is *that* supposed to mean?"

Keegel Farzym sighed. "How long Always October has existed is a mystery; we know neither where it came from, nor how it came to be, though our poets and magicians have many theories. My own belief is that we are a reflection of your world—that we monsters are, in some strange way, a creation of you humans.

"Like all reflections, we show ourselves in reverse. This means that the worst of us are formed from the dark side of truly wonderful human beings, while the best of us are reflections of people who would be called monsters in your world no matter how they looked."

He spit out another bone. Little Dumpling snatched it before it hit the ground and began to chew on it.

"So. We have good monsters and bad monsters, just as you have good people and bad people, and things are pretty much in balance. But something is happening here that could disturb that balance, both in our world, and in yours."

I pulled the bone away from Little Dumpling,

who growled but didn't bite, and hoisted him onto my shoulders. He looked at the moon and howled.

In the distance something howled back.

"I'm not sure I understand what you're talking about," I said.

Keegel Farzym frowned—an awesome sight, given his face—and began to walk once more. I followed him, stepping around a steaming puddle.

"I lead a group that believes monsters and humans are part of the same family. We are opposed by a group of monsters who disagree. This group is seeking to unweave the Great Magic that binds our worlds together, to sever the threads that connect us." He paused and sucked his lower lip. "How can I explain this? It would be as if our worlds were getting a divorce."

The word made me shiver; my parents' divorce was the worst time of my life.

"How can you divorce a whole world?" I asked. "And why would they want to do that?"

Keegel Farzym lifted Little Dumpling from my shoulders and hoisted him into the air, a good twelve feet above the ground. Little Dumpling laughed and tried to grab the moon.

Keeping his eyes on the baby, Keegel Farzym said, "They say they do not want to be a reflection of anyone. They want to be totally independent. This may be possible; personally, I don't think it is. I believe we are all connected, and this magic would be fatal for both worlds. We are woven of the same stuff, Jason, you and I, your world and mine. We are like the front and the back of a tapestry. Try to separate one side from the other, and you destroy the whole."

Lowering Little Dumpling, he tucked him into the crook of his arm and chucked him under the chin the way my mother liked to do. L.D. gurgled happily and blew a spit bubble.

"Besides," said Keegel Farzym, gazing fondly at the baby, "without humans, what would little monsters dream of to frighten them during the day?"

V. The Price

We came to a giant tree with a door in its trunk. Keegel Farzym told me to stand close to the tree. Then he walked around it in a wide circle, muttering to himself.

"You and the prince wait here," he said at last. "Do not cross this line. I must go and clear the way for us. Be careful. Speak to no one."

I took Little Dumpling's hand and nodded. Keegel Farzym opened the door, ducked his head, and disappeared into the tree.

I was alone in Monster Land. Well, I had Little Dumpling. But he was just a baby, and a monster to boot. So I felt pretty nervous. I got even more nervous when eyes began to appear in the darkness around us, glowing eyes that hung at all levels, as if the creatures they belonged to stood anywhere from a foot to twelve feet tall.

Then a flickering light, not an eye, began approaching us. Soon I could see that it came from a torch.

When the torchbearer finally came into sight, I was overwhelmed by astonishment—and relief. It was my father! My father!

"Jason, thank goodness I found you!" he cried. "Come on—bring the baby and we'll go home."

Clutching Little Dumpling's hand, I started toward my father. I wondered how he had managed to track us here.

I had not taken more than three or four steps when the door in the tree opened and Keegel Farzym reappeared. "Jason!" he roared. "What are you doing?"

"I'm getting out of here!" I said, picking up Little Dumpling and running toward my dad.

"Jason, don't cross that line!" yelled Keegel Farzym.

I didn't slow down.

"Jason, that's *not* your father!"

Now I did slow down. It had to be my father, standing there beneath that tree.

It *had* to be.

But then, if it was him, why didn't he come and get me, instead of just standing there?

"Jason, hurry up," said Dad, his voice urgent.

I took a step forward.

"Jason, if you leave the circle, I can't protect you!" cried Keegel Farzym.

I hesitated again.

"Hurry, Jason," said Dad. "I can't come and get you. He has that ring sealed against me."

"How do you know that?" I asked.

"I just do. Now hurry."

I took a step backward.

"Hurry!" he snarled.

I took another step back.

"Hurry, damn you!" As the words flew out, his face changed. Clothes splitting, he exploded into Mazrak, the monster who had been lurking in my closet.

Keegel Farzym grabbed me from behind and dragged me and Little Dumpling through the door in the tree. He waited for me to stop crying before moving on.

We walked down a long spiral stair dimly lit by glowing fungus.

"Mazrak is the chief operative of the enemy," said Keegel Farzym. "He wants to keep the prince from returning to your world."

"Why?"

"Because if Dum Pling is in your world, the Great Unraveling cannot work. The prince acts as a knot, tying our worlds together. That is why he was taken there to begin with. His mother is the wife of King Bork, who leads the faction that wants to split the worlds. She disagreed with her husband and brought the prince to your world to stop the Unraveling. It was a dangerous journey, and she undertook it to save both worlds. Alas, she acted hastily, and without our help."

Though he said nothing more, the tone of his voice made me think that Little Dumpling's mother had not made it back alive.

"Where are we going now?" I asked.

"You must speak to the Council of Poets," replied Keegel Farzym. "Then, you must make a choice."

We entered a large chamber. It was lit by flickering torches. Twisting roots—some fine as a hair, some thicker than my arm—thrust through the ceiling and the moist, earthen walls. Patches of toadstools dotted the floor. In the distance I could hear a waterfall.

"Pretty! Hello!" cried Little Dumpling when he saw the six monsters facing us. They sat in a half circle around a wooden table. At the center of the half circle was an empty chair, large and carved with strange designs.

While not one of the monsters looked like any of the others, they all had three things in common: They were large, they were strange, and they were scary.

"Welcome back, Keegel Farzym," said the monster farthest to the right, who seemed to be a lady. "Congratulations on your safe return."

Keegel Farzym nodded to her. Then, after patting both me and Little Dumpling on the head, he walked around the table and took his place in the large chair at the center of the group. Looking me straight in the eye, he said, "Jason Burger, our two worlds, the world of humans and the world of monsters, are in terrible danger. Are you willing to try to save them?"

"*Me?*" I squeaked. "What can I do? I'm just a kid."

"You can care for this child, who is our hope for the future."

I looked at Little Dumpling. He smiled up at me, showing his fangs.

"As long as he is in your world, then your world and ours will be bound together, and the Great Unraveling can be prevented. Should he be stolen and brought back here—or should he perish, perish the thought—then the end will begin. We do not know why his mother brought him to you of all humans. Was it choice? Accident? Fate? It does not matter. When the moment comes to decide what you will do for your world, the question is not 'Why me?' It is simply 'Can I, *will* I, do it?' "

"Up," said Little Dumpling, holding out his arms.

"I never wanted a little brother," I said, even as I was hoisting him.

"Who does?" said the slimy green creature sitting at the far left of the group. It winked at me with an eye the size of a baseball.

"Little brothers can be a terrible annoyance," added the gaunt figure next to him. I could not see this monster's face, for it was hidden by the hood of its long black robe.

"True," said the lady monster at the other end of the table. "But then, so can first children. And what would happen if parents never bothered to have them, either?"

"All right, all right," I said. "I'll take care of him. I kind of like the little guy anyway. What do I have to do?"

"All that you would normally do," said Keegel Farzym, "plus this: You must take this amulet and place it about his neck."

He rummaged under his beard for a moment, then held out his hand. In the center of his huge blue palm rested a metal disk engraved with a strange design. It was attached to a golden chain. I stared at it. A shiver of fear I did not understand rippled through me.

"Will you take it?" he asked after a time. "Will you place it about his neck?"

"Can't you do it?" I asked. My throat was dry, and my words came out in little more than a whisper.

Keegel Farzym shook his head. "It must be the hand of a human that places it about the baby's neck."

After setting Little Dumpling on the floor, I stepped forward and took the amulet from the hand of the High Poet of the Land of Always October. But as I moved to place it around the baby's neck, Keegel Farzym said, "Wait! Before you do this, you must know one more thing. You must know what it will cost you."

I didn't like the sound of that.

"What do you mean?" I asked nervously.

"No magic comes without a price," said the shaggy, dark-eyed creature sitting at Keegel Farzym's right hand. "This, too, is part of the Weaving."

Keegel Farzym put his hand on my shoulder. It was heavy. "Dum Pling displays his true form in your world when the moon is full. Because he is but an infant, he cannot control this aspect of himself. At the next full moon he will once again transform. The energy this transformation releases will reveal his location to the monsters who wish to return him to *this* world." He paused, then said, "This amulet will collect that transforming energy as it builds throughout the month."

I was beginning to have a bad feeling about this. "And what happens to that energy when the full moon comes?" I asked.

"On that night you must take the amulet from Dum Pling and place it about your own neck."

"I think I can guess what will happen," I muttered.

Keegel Farzym nodded. "*You* will become a monster."

"Won't they find us anyway?" I asked. "For that matter, don't they know where we are already?"

"The answer to your first question is no; your human aura will mask and mingle with Dum Pling's monster energy, creating a mixture that is confused and less likely to be tracked.

"As to your second question"—he paused, then spread his huge arms—"we are doing our best to find Mazrak. If we can capture him, it is unlikely anyone else will come after you. On this I can make no promise; danger is part of the bargain. However, I can offer a promise of help, and protection. Your closet, like most closets, and nearly all mirrors, can be a gate between your world and the Land of Always October. We will guard that gate. We will watch over you. We will always be nearby in case of trouble."

I looked at them.

I stared at Little Dumpling.

I thought of how my life had unraveled when my mother and father divorced.

Lifting the chain, I dropped it over the baby's neck.

* * *

There isn't much more to tell—at least not yet. Once I had made my decision, Keegel Farzym took us down a long tunnel. We stepped into a pool of blue light, and next thing I knew we were walking out of my closet and into my room.

The big monster held Little Dumpling for a moment. A tear fell from his eye to the baby's forehead.

"Good night, little prince," he whispered sadly. "Good night and good-bye, my grandson."

Turning, he stepped into my closet and disappeared.

I lifted Little Dumpling, who was now completely human in form, and placed him in the crib. I handed him his rattle, then tucked the blanket my mother had just that day finished weaving for him up to his chin. When he was asleep, I went to the window and stared into the darkness.

The world out there was stranger, more frightening, and far more interesting than I had ever guessed.

Suddenly it also seemed very fragile.

Returning to the crib, I folded down the blanket and touched Little Dumpling's amulet. I would have to do some fast talking to convince my mother to leave it on him.

I would be doing a lot of fast talking over the next few years.

I lifted the amulet on two fingertips. It was light as a feather. Yet once a month, when I hung it around my own neck, it would carry the weight of the world—the weight of two worlds that were one.

I went back to the window, thrust my head into the night, and began to howl at the moon.

I figured I might as well start practicing.

Little kids have the weirdest imaginations. . . .

MOMSTER IN THE CLOSET

Jane Yolen

"There's a momster in my closet," Kenny said. "I heard him this morning."

"Grumpf ouff," Dad said, his mouth full.

"That's nice, dear. Do you want more?" Mom asked.

You see, with Kenny it was something new in that closet every day. At five—"And a half!" he'd be quick to remind you—he had more imagination than sense. Also, he watched too much TV.

"Come on, squirt," I said, "or we'll be late." I took an extra-long swallow as Kenny shrugged into his backpack. He followed me out the door.

"Was, too, a momster," he said.

"Monster," I corrected automatically.

"With long grungy hair. And weird claws. He was nine feet . . . no, ten feet tall."

"Heard all that through the door?" I asked.

That shut him up. Of course, last week it had

been a weirdwolf. The time before it had been a ghould. He didn't know how to pronounce the stuff, but he was convinced they were all there. That must be *some* closet, I thought, and said so out loud.

"Right to Momster Land," Kenny said.

Kids! I could hardly recall ever being that young. It felt as if I had been a teenager forever.

When we got home, the sun was sitting just below the horizon. Summers are hard around here. There is just not enough night.

"Come on, squirt," I said. "Time for bed."

"I don't want to go," Kenny said. "There's a momster in the closet."

"You have to. I have to. That's the way of the world," I said. "Besides, it's monster. Spelled with an *n*, not an *m*."

"It's got spells, too?" Kenny said. "Oh, no—it will *really* get me."

"There's nothing there," I said, my patience beginning to go. "Besides, if it threatens you, just growl back at it and show your teeth like this." I bared my fangs at him.

Kenny giggled.

We went inside. Mom was already settled down, but Dad was still up, sitting in front of the TV and watching the flag flapping in time to the National Anthem. It's only a little more exciting than a test pattern. He didn't seem to hear us.

Kenny and I went into the room we shared, and I helped him get undressed. He still has trouble with the knots in his shoelaces. I keep asking Mom to find him a pair of Velcro sneakers.

Once we were in our pajamas and had brushed our teeth, he raced ahead of me to his bed. He turned for a moment and growled at the closet.

"Fangs for the memory," I said.

He giggled again, though I don't think he got the joke.

"Last one in is a . . ." he shouted.

". . . rotten . . ." I prompted.

". . . corpse!" He made a funny face and lay down. Once his eyes were closed, he was very still.

I kissed his forehead, moving aside the hair as white-gold as corn silk, and tenderly closed the lid over him. Then I climbed into my own coffin, pulling it shut before the first light of day could come streaming through the blinds. Monsters in the closet, indeed! Kenny knew, as I did, that only sunlight or a stake through the heart can really kill a vampire.

I closed my eyes and slept.

Before anyone but the wizard Merlin knew his real identity, the boy who was to become King Arthur was fostered out to the care of Sir Ector. Here is one adventure that Arthur and his foster brother Cai (in some stories known as Kay) might have had on their way to becoming knights. . . .

MERLIN'S KNIGHT SCHOOL

Michael Markiewicz

My little brother Arthur and I had walked nearly ten miles to see our godfather, Merlin, the sorcerer, when we had a slight mishap. We had left home early in the morning to continue the training he had promised, but hadn't counted on a soaking rain, which made the path slippery and slow. We knew the way quite well, having made the trip at least ten times that year, and got thoroughly bored by the afternoon.

Arthur decided to liven things up by showing me how well he could climb the slick boulders that lined the path. Naturally he fell into a huge patch of nettles. The stinging vines quickly wrapped around him as he thrashed and screamed, and he was soon hopelessly tangled. Arthur was good for this sort of thing. He had a lot of courage for such a small kid, but he wasn't all that bright.

"Help! Cai! I've fallen in the briers," he wailed. "Get me out!"

"Those aren't briers," explained Merlin, who suddenly appeared in the path ahead of us like a ghost out of the fog. "They're nettles."

"Ow!" Arthur screamed. "I don't care what they are, just get me out of here!"

Merlin walked calmly over to Arthur and eyed the situation, seeming both amused and annoyed. He wasn't really angry. If he were angry, he would have given Arthur "The Look."

"You wouldn't have gotten tangled if you hadn't panicked," Merlin chided.

"Well, I'm stuck now!"

"Close your eyes," Merlin ordered. He then poured some dust from a small bag and recited a strange poem.

Arthur fidgeted nervously and then out of nowhere came a flash of fire. It filled the brush where Arthur lay and flared like a small raging sun. As it rumbled and cracked, I heard Arthur scream, and I wondered if Merlin had lost his senses and killed the boy. The fire quickly burned out, leaving the vines brown and brittle. I was relieved when I saw, through the smoke, that Arthur was untouched and it was only the nettles that had been charred to a crisp.

"Wow!" shouted Arthur, who easily broke free of the blackened mass. "Why don't you do that to all the nettles? Then people wouldn't get stuck in them."

"Hmmph," snorted the wizard. "Your comfort isn't the most important thing in the world."

"Huh?"

"Oh, never mind," he replied as he shooed a rabbit from the burned undergrowth and chased it into the brush on the other side of the path.

Merlin's hovel sat at the base of a large hill. It overlooked a beautiful valley, whose only flaw was that almost all of the lakes within it were choked with reeds and wild grass. One lake, however, had somehow been transformed by the wizard into a shining crystal-clear wonder. That lake was the reason the people of Parridge allowed a wizard to keep his home in the area.

Merlin's house, like a two-headed goat, had its own sense of charm. Its window was hung with drying herbs, and interesting smells confronted one with every turn. Spices lined the walls. Balls and boxes and twisted metal shapes covered the floor. The furniture, consisting of two wooden chairs, a bed, and two tables, was nearly buried in the disarray.

We arrived at Merlin's house late in the evening and stumbled inside over the piles of debris. We were anxious to continue our lessons. Merlin had been helping us prepare to become squires, and we were both in a hurry to complete the training that we had started almost a year and a half earlier.

Before we got down to business, however, he offered us some food. It smelled pretty bad, and it was hard to tell exactly what it was, but we were hungry and ate it anyway. We were probably better off not knowing what it was, and only a fool would insult a wizard's cooking. Merlin turned to us after our less-than-delicious dinner with a slight smile.

"Becoming a squire is your second step toward becoming a knight. You have learned enough to become pages. Now you must begin the hard road toward becoming a servant of the king. You must both become as wise and as strong as the greatest knight."

I looked down at Arthur, who was picking bits of food out of his lap, and thought that Merlin might actually be insane.

As the magician rambled on, I looked out the tiny window and noticed someone running up the long walk.

"Merlin, help!" cried a large man, who burst through the doorway, sending baubles and trinkets flying. "Master Merlin," he pleaded, "our daughter is dying. Please come and help her."

Merlin turned to the man with a look of amazement. "I'm not a healer! Go get—"

"Please! We already asked Grandmother Kirneas, but she couldn't help the fever. Now I think she'll die for sure. You cured that lake; surely you can do some magic for our girl."

Muttering to himself, Merlin grabbed one of the books that had been buried under a pile of parchment and turned toward us. "You two will have to stay here," he said roughly. "I don't want you getting this sickness. And keep out of trouble. Do you understand?"

"We won't get into anything," I assured him.

We watched Merlin and the man run down the path toward the village until they disappeared in the darkness. I turned to Arthur, who already had a wicked grin on his face, and said, "What are we waiting for? Let's find something to get into!"

Arthur began rooting in the boxes under the table while I inspected the tools and metal things. One, in particular, a large glove with razor-sharp spikes on the fingers and back, seemed quite deadly. I put it in my pouch, figuring it might be useful in case any unwelcome visitors showed up in Merlin's absence.

Suddenly Arthur yelped. Well, not exactly a yelp—more like a "Ca—mmph—oooooooo," followed by a thud. I wasn't worried until I turned to see what he had gotten into and couldn't find him. I wondered, would Merlin turn us into bugs just for going through his stuff?

I was somewhat relieved when I heard Arthur cry, "Help! Cai! I'm in a hole!"

In a hole? Now I was curious. Sure enough, at

the bottom of one of the piles Arthur had found a trapdoor. Naturally, he had opened it. Underneath was a ten-foot-deep pit. Still following the course of nature, he had fallen into it.

"Hold on," I said. "I'll climb down and get you out."

I found a rope in the mess on the floor and carefully tied it to one of the heavy tables. As I stepped down into the pit, however, my brilliant brother grabbed the rope and pulled. I teetered on the edge for a moment. Then the huge table suddenly slid across the room, smacked me in the side, and sent me plummeting into the darkness.

For a moment I thought I was dead. Dazed and dizzy, I felt as if I were spinning in the blackness of hell. Then, slowly, I began to come to my senses.

"Arthur, are we alive?"

"Yes."

"Am I hanging upside down on the rope?"

"Yes."

"Is the table blocking the hole and cutting off all the light?"

"Yes."

Thud!

"Did the rope just break?"

"Mmphess! Gmmet awwf meeee!"

After sorting things out, and reshaping my head into a rough oval, I managed to make a small fire with my trusty flint and some pieces of the broken table. It was only then that we realized there was another way out. The pit had an entrance to a downward sloping tunnel.

We peered into the gloom of the passageway.

"What do you suppose is down there?" asked Arthur quietly.

"Probably nothing," I replied, not wanting to tell him what I really thought.

With little opportunity to get out the way we came in, we began our descent into the blackness. As we twisted down through a long, narrow passage, we suddenly found ourselves entering a large cave. It was a huge circular area with walls at least seventy feet high. In the center of the cave was a small pond surrounded by a muddy shore. The water was probably an underground spring that connected to the lake nearby.

Just enough light filtered through a crack in the high ceiling for us to make out some of the other contents of the room. A huge pile of greenish slime with a pitchfork stuck in it filled one corner, and there was something we could not quite make out near the edge of the water. Cautiously we moved toward the pond until we saw that it was a box about the size of—*a coffin!*

At first I thought the noise I heard was the bones of some undead horror springing from the box. But then Arthur said, "Cai, close your mouth; your teeth are chattering."

"Should we open the thing?" I asked.

"Sure, as soon as I become king, I'll do just that."

It was possible that there was something inside that could get us out of the pit. Besides, I figured things couldn't get much worse. So, with all the courage I could muster, I gently lifted the lid.

The box didn't contain a body. That would have been merciful. Instead, lying inside was what looked like a wooden sword. Arthur's eyes lit up as soon as he saw the toy blade. He grabbed the wooden shaft and before I could do anything said those wretched words, "I wish . . ."

Now, my father had always said, "Be careful what you wish for; you might get it." But he never said anything about someone else's wishes. Arthur couldn't have turned a better phrase had he been coached by Aladdin, or better yet, Pandora.

"I wish I could fight something with this sword."

Notice he said "fight," not "defeat," not "kill," not "maim seriously and walk away." No, he just said "fight." And so it was.

Suddenly the ground began to shake. The large pool of water started to ripple and spurt like a boiling kettle. Arthur and I, terrified by the increasing rumble, looked blankly at the water's edge as something large—very, very, *very* large— shot straight up out of the pool and began to whirl around the room. It looked like a giant snake, maybe thirty feet long, but there was no head that we could see, only a long, smooth, black body that moved faster than lightning.

It also stank. In fact, it smelled so bad that I began to appreciate the odor of Merlin's food—anything was better than this stench. Unfortunately, the food in my stomach didn't mix well with the smell, and I soon wished I had skipped dinner.

As I dropped to my knees in one corner of the room and deposited Merlin's feast on the cave floor, I noticed that Arthur had started chasing the giant thing. He was swinging his fake weapon and screaming like a lunatic. Unfortunately, I was in no condition to tell him just how stupid that looked; a wooden sword wouldn't pop a pimple on this thing.

I quickly composed myself and ran after him but was too late. Out of the water slithered another giant snake. It wrapped around his legs, then lifted his tiny body into the air. He beat its hide with the useless sword but did little damage. I ran to the edge of the water as Arthur was tossed about the room like a small doll.

I looked into the pond to see if I could find some weak point. Instead, I saw an even worse terror. This wasn't a pair of giant creatures. They were merely two arms, two out of at least seven or eight, that were attached to an even more gigantic thing that filled the whole pond! It looked like a big slimy spider—deep black and at least seventy feet long. In the middle of it was a huge mouth with several long tongues. Just above its mouth was a single huge eye, which now seemed to be looking right at me.

As I stared in disbelief at the enormous thing, I was swept off my feet by one of the arms. I tried to break its hold on my legs but could barely tell which way was up. It spun me around and around. Twice I saw Arthur in the confusion as the beast twirled us in the air. My brother looked as though he might pass out at any moment, and I thought that we would surely die.

It bashed us against the walls. Then it slowly began to lower me to the water's surface. Arthur brandished his little sword and screamed that he wouldn't let it eat me. But I knew it could do anything it darn well pleased. I looked down to see the giant's mouth open, ready to swallow me headfirst. The mouth extended its tongues, poised to wrap around my face and draw me in. Then, suddenly, I remembered the glove I had taken from the hovel. Frantically I pulled it from the pouch and tried to hack at one of the tongues.

The long sinewy lickers simply wrapped around the glove and tore it from my hand. I watched, in total defeat, as it swallowed the weapon whole. Then a small miracle happened.

The beast started to loosen its grip. It must

have been injured as it bit down on the glove's razor points. Distracted for the moment, it let both of us fall into the water.

I made for shore, then turned to see if Arthur had followed me. I watched in horror as he dived down and lunged for the thing with his toy sword. He poked at the thing like a flea on a rabid wolf. I looked around wildly for some kind of weapon and saw the pitchfork. Grabbing the long handle, I jumped into the water again. I tried to stab the beast but was quickly disarmed as one of the tentacles grabbed my hands. Now I was sure we were finished.

The beast pulled me underwater. It was drawing me toward its mouth again. I looked into the open jaws and saw its teeth ready to close on my arms. Fighting to hold my breath, I tried not to scream. Now I could see right down into its grisly black throat. I realized then that I was about to become its dinner.

Suddenly I felt it jerk and tear away. Through the dark pool I looked up and saw the monster's eye oozing as if it had been struck. Looking around to find Arthur, I saw him swimming near the surface. He had speared the thing. He must have hit it fairly well, judging from the flow of black blood that quickly filled the pond.

Its arms thrashed wildly for a few moments and then, mercifully, fell lifeless along the edges of the dark room. While it died Arthur and I crawled out of the slimy dark liquid.

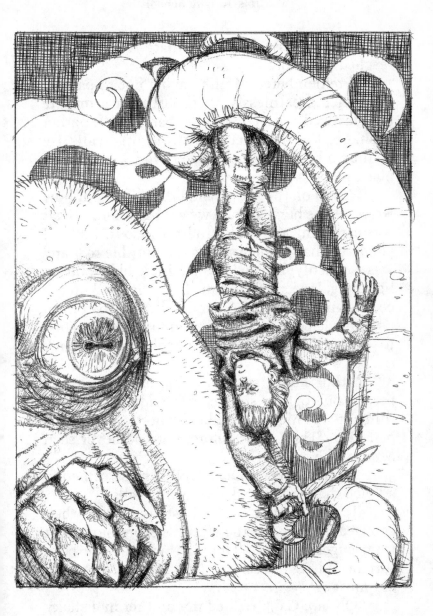

"Arthur, how did you do that?" I asked as we reached the shore.

"I remembered Merlin saying not to panic!" he replied breathlessly. "I thought for a minute and realized . . . I could probably get another wish. So, I wished that the sword was real!" He held up a brilliant steel blade covered with thick black blood.

We fell on the shore, and I thought about how we would be heroes when we got back home. That was assuming we could find a way out. But as I pondered that problem, I heard a horrible roar and was suddenly blinded by an incredible bolt of lightning. It seemed to come from the crack in the ceiling and struck the ground only a few feet from us. It made both of us nearly blind and deaf. Then it fizzled, leaving a thick column of black smoke.

Arthur and I sat trembling as a figure appeared out of the smoke. It could only be one thing. It was Merlin, and he did not look happy. I had seen "The Look" before, but had never seen Merlin like this.

"WHAT HAVE YOU DONE!" he screamed in a voice that shook rocks from the walls.

"I killed that . . ." I started, but then changed my mind as the wizard's expression went from anger to rage. "Um . . . actually we both sort of did it. I mean . . . actually . . . Arthur did most—"

"Oh, no, Cai," replied my brother in a shaky

voice. "No, you can take the credit. I didn't even help, really."

"But . . . I don't understand," I stammered. "That thing . . . we had to kill it. It was going to kill us."

"Do you know how long it took me to conjure one of those? To train it? To . . . ARGH!" His bellow shook the floor and sent ripples on the black water. "Do you know the lake on this side of the valley?" he asked.

"Yes."

"Can you guess what cleaned up that lake so that the people could use it?"

Suddenly I realized why Merlin was so angry —he had used the beast to clean the lake!

"Oh . . . Merlin, I'm sorry. I'm really—"

"Never mind the apologies. . . . I ought to have you two go out and scoop up the weeds by hand."

I didn't like the sound of that and quickly came up with a brilliant alternative. "Say," I proposed, "why can't Arthur just use that magic sword to wish all the weeds away?"

Merlin scowled, and then Arthur replied with an unusual burst of insight, "No . . . if we just wish away things we wind up with other problems. There might be fish or something that needs some weeds to live in." I had never known Arthur to be very bright, but suddenly, just for a moment, he seemed intelligent—almost wise.

"In fact," said the sorcerer, trying to hide a

very small smile, "I used some of those very weeds to help save that girl's life this evening. It was the only thing that could break her fever. But I am proud of you, Arthur, for realizing that. And I suppose some of this is my fault for not repairing that rickety trapdoor. If I had, you wouldn't have gotten down here in the first place."

The wizard sighed as he inspected the giant corpse.

Arthur spoke softly. "We really are sorry, Merlin, we just didn't—"

"I know. Well, what's done is done. Now you just have to take the responsibility for it."

"What does that mean?" I asked, picturing the rest of my life spent in a small boat yanking slimy vines from the wizard's lake.

Merlin thought for a moment and then ordered, "You two will clean up this mess. Then you will help me conjure another beast from the spring."

I moaned as my stomach began to ache from the thought.

"Then you will spend the next three months helping me train it to clean the lake. You'll get used to the smell eventually."

I gagged and began to whimper.

Then he patted his ribs and said happily, "But first, we should get something to eat. How about if we finish that stew I made earlier today?"

I cried.

*This strange and moving story talks about a
different kind of monster. There is more going on
here than you might first realize. . . .*

UNCLE JOSHUA AND
THE GROOGLEMEN

Debra Doyle and James D. Macdonald

*"In the First Year came the Plague, and in the
Tenth Year the Burning, and afterwards came
the Grooglemen out of the Dead Lands. . . ."*

—*A History of the New World From the
Beginning to the Present Day*
by Absolom Steerforth, Speaker of the
Amity Crossroads Assembly

* * *

*Groogleman, groogleman,
Take one in three.
Groogleman, groogleman,
Don't take me.*
—Children's counting-out rhyme,
Foothills District

* * *

Daniel Henchard was sixteen and a bit, and Leezie Johnson was almost fourteen when the grooglemen came down out of the mountains into the new-settled country.

The grooglemen came between hay-making and harvesttime, on a moonless night when the lightning flashed and the thunder boomed across the hills. In the dawn a column of smoke rose from the Johnson homestead off to the east. Those of the Henchards who were eating breakfast in the kitchen saw the smoke and made up their minds to go have a look. They would see the trouble and help if they could, for the Henchards and the Johnsons were kin as well as neighbors.

The Johnson place was more than an hour away to run, and longer at a walk. It was mid-morning before the farmhouse came into view, and what the Henchards saw then was as bad as could be. The whole house was burnt, and the ashes gone white from burning out without being quenched—the outbuildings, too, and never a sight of living man or beast.

The farmyard told the rest of the story: nine burned patches in a straight row, nine tidy black rectangles on the hard-packed earth, and in each rectangle a lump of burnt bone and blackened meat. Dan Henchard said later that you could tell which one was which, almost—the big one would have been Rafe, who was tall, and at the end of the row, the little patch no more than two feet long and half that wide, that one would have been the baby. Its bones were gone entirely.

"The grooglemen," said Aunt Min Henchard.

"There's only nine here," Sam Henchard said. He was the oldest of the Henchard brothers, and Dan's father. "There were ten Johnsons."

"Sometimes the grooglemen take one back with them to their castle," said Bartolmy Henchard—Aunt Min's husband and Sam's brother. "There's worse things than being dead, and that's one of them. I hear sometimes the grooglemen get hungry."

"Who is it that's missing?" asked young Dan Henchard.

"Leezie," said Uncle Joshua. He'd been standing by, saying nothing, for that was his way. "I feared that if the grooglemen came, it's her that they'd take. And now, there's none of her size here," he said, nodding at the row.

Uncle Joshua wasn't anyone's blood uncle, but a wanderer who'd come by the Henchard farm one day two winters gone, traveling on foot from some place farther north. He wasn't much of a farmer, but when he went off into the woods for a day or a week at a time with his long flintlock rifle, he always came back with meat. He brought in more than enough food to earn his keep, and in the evenings by the fireside he told marvelous stories of distant lands.

So he stayed on and became a part of the family by courtesy if not in fact, for all he was much younger than any of Father's brothers. Aunt Min said he was only waiting for Leezie Johnson to grow old enough for a husband, and then they'd both be off to whatever foreign place it was whose accent still marked Joshua's speech. Dan Henchard had always hoped that Min was wrong, because Leezie had been like a sister to him while they were young, and he would miss her sorely if she grew up to marry an outlander and leave the settlement. But even that was better than being dead—or a prisoner of the grooglemen.

"We have to bury them," Sam Henchard said.

"You bury them," said Uncle Joshua. "I'm off to find the girl."

"You can't," Aunt Min told him. "You're a hunter, but the grooglemen leave no footprints to trace. They fly through the air by night."

"Min's right," said Bartolmy. "The grooglemen see in the dark, and you can't hide from them. No one has ever been to their castle and come back down again."

"That's where you're wrong," said Uncle Joshua. The outlands accent was strong in his words. "One man at least has been to their stronghold and come back, for I've done it."

"Then there's never a man done it twice!" Bartolmy said. "And when they find where you've come from, they'll follow you back and kill us, too."

Uncle Joshua shook his head. "They'll not trace me."

"How can you say that?" said Aunt Min. "Everybody knows that when a groogleman asks you a question, you have to tell him the truth. Can't help yourself."

But Uncle Joshua only slung his rifle over his shoulder and said, "What's worse—being taken by the grooglemen or knowing that nobody will ever come to win you back?"

No one answered. Dan Henchard said afterward that his father, Sam, looked sad and ashamed, but Bartolmy and Aunt Min never so much as blinked an eye.

So Dan said to Uncle Joshua, "I'll come with you," because he understood what the answer to the question was. It was worse, far worse, to be abandoned.

Uncle Joshua frowned at him. "You don't know what you're saying. Stay home with your father."

"Walk beside you or follow behind you," said Dan, "it makes no difference to me. I'm no safer at home than on the road."

"As you will."

Uncle Joshua turned without a further word and walked off to the north, and Dan walked beside him.

The two walked a long way, over hills and through a mountain gap, past where Dan had ever heard of anyone going, or anyone coming from. For eight days they walked.

"Whatever was going to happen to Leezie has happened by now," Dan said. "She's dead for sure."

Uncle Joshua looked at him with an angry expression. "If you want to go home, go now and never let me see your face again. Tomorrow, or the next day at the last, we'll pass beyond the living lands, and then it will be too late to turn back."

They went on; but it was two more days, not one, before they crossed over the border into the dead lands.

Dan could see why the name was given. The ground here was jumbled and broken stone, and the trees were stunted and misshapen where they grew at all. The sounds of birds and tracks of beasts were left behind as well. The air itself smelled dead, like the taste of licking metal.

At the end of the first day Dan asked, "Is it like this much longer?"

"Don't talk," Uncle Joshua said. "The grooglemen can hear you."

They didn't light a fire in the dark that night, nor was there food beyond what was in their pouches, gathered in the days when they'd been walking through fertile country. The next morning they journeyed onward—but they walked warily, and if Uncle Joshua had moved like a hunter before, now he moved doubly so and at times vanished from Dan's sight altogether.

And then, without warning, a vast rushing sound filled the air. Dan looked about wildly for help, but Uncle Joshua was nowhere to be seen. Dan cowered beside a rock that rose slab-sided out of the barren dirt, and when he lifted his head again, a groogleman stood before him.

The groogleman had a wrinkled skin all dirty white like fungus, and huge glistening eyes over a round and wrinkled mouth. It shuffled when it walked, and Dan could hear it breathing—a loud hissing noise like a teakettle on the hearth. The creature took Dan and bound him and carried him over hard and blackened fields to the castle of the grooglemen, where the great gate shut behind them.

Then the groogleman laid its misshapen hands on Dan's shoulders and looked him full in the face and spoke; and Dan couldn't understand a word of what it said.

The dungeon cells beneath the castle were carved each from a solid piece of stone, and the air was full of whispers of far-off voices speaking too low to be understood. The groogleman took Dan there and left him. Though he was not bound, he felt no desire to escape, and in the small part of his mind that was still his own he knew he was under a spell.

He didn't move, even when the groogleman

put out a claw and tasted his blood, and he didn't try to run when the groogleman left him and the door stayed open. Nor did he move when the groogleman returned and—in a voice that was harsh and strangely accented—asked him from where he came and why.

Dan tried to remain silent. But he answered every question that was put to him, and told of Leezie, of Uncle Joshua, of the Henchard farm, of his family and his friends. Nothing was secret, and the groogleman was quiet except for its hissing and gurgling breath as it listened.

But what wasn't asked, the spell couldn't force Dan to betray. So the groogleman never asked or learned that Dan expected Uncle Joshua to come to Leezie's rescue, and to his.

The dungeon of the grooglemen was never dark—the light there was cold and unnatural, coming from torches that burned without smoke and never seemed to flicker or be diminished—but at last Dan slept. When he awoke, Uncle Joshua was standing at his feet.

"You've come," Dan said.

Uncle Joshua put his finger to his lips and helped Dan to stand. They went out of the cell into a corridor lit by the weird pale fires, going past open doors and closed doors and colored lines and paintings of black and yellow flowers. The wind sighed around them and brought to their ears the muttering of far-off voices.

"How did you find me?" Dan asked as they went.

"You've not been here long," Uncle Joshua whispered back. "Finding you was easy. It's Leezie will be hard to find. Did you see her—or did the groogleman tell of her?"

"No," said Dan.

"Then it's up to us to find her. Can you walk faster?"

Dan nodded.

"Come on, then," Uncle Joshua told him. "We'll live as long as we're not seen."

"Are we going home without Leezie?"

"No," said Uncle Joshua.

They went on deeper into the castle, with Uncle Joshua walking a little way ahead, watching in all directions. He carried his rifle in both hands across his chest, with the hammer back and the flint poised above the pan like a wild animal's sharp fang.

"Can grooglemen be killed?" Dan asked.

"We may yet find out," Uncle Joshua said. "Now hush and help me search for Leezie. If she lives, it will be our doing."

And so they walked for a long time, silent, through the maze of rooms and corridors and halls, up stairs and down ramps, in the castle of the grooglemen. Some doors were open, some were locked, and at last they came to a place where they heard a girl's voice weeping.

Uncle Joshua held up his hand to call a halt

and began to step carefully forward. Slowly he looked around the corner of the passageway, then gestured for Dan to come join him. He'd found a door, and the weeping voice was on the other side. But the door was locked, and it had neither latch nor keyhole.

"What now?" Dan asked.

"We'll see," said Uncle Joshua, and cried out in a loud voice, "Leezie, is that you?"

The weeping stopped. "Who is it?" came a girl's voice from the other side of the door.

"It's us!" Dan called. "Dan Henchard and Uncle Joshua. We're here to bring you home."

"Get away!" Leezie shouted back. "Get away before it's too late for you. It's too late for me already. The grooglemen can see me here. They'll see you, too, if you stay."

"Open the door!"

"I can't. There's a spell on it. Only a groogleman can pass through."

"The groogleman," Uncle Joshua muttered. "He'll let you out. Leezie—call the groogleman! Call him loud. Call him now."

"No!"

"Yes! He gave you words to say to bring him. Say them now."

"How do you know what the groogleman did?" Dan asked.

"I *know*," Uncle Joshua replied. "Come now."

He walked back to the corner and sat against the wall where he could look in both directions. There he waited, and Dan Henchard waited with him, until at length a shuffling noise sounded in the corridor.

Then the groogleman appeared, walking its slow and clumsy walk, its feet barely clearing the floor and its head moving from side to side as it looked about.

Uncle Joshua stood and raised his rifle to his shoulder. "Stand where you are!"

The groogleman seemed to see Uncle Joshua for the first time. It halted, and its massive head shook slowly from side to side. There was no expression in its blank eyes, and its tight, wrinkled mouth never moved. But the hissing of its breath stopped, and its hands, with their fat white fingers extended, rose up to the level of the groogleman's thick waist as if to push Uncle Joshua away.

Uncle Joshua jerked his head in the direction of the closed door. "Open it."

The groogleman shook its head again.

The rifle fired. A flash of white smoke rose up from the pan and a cloud of smoke came out of the barrel, and a noise like a thunderclap echoed in the cold stone hall. Uncle Joshua didn't pause. He slung the rifle back on his shoulder and dashed forward, even as the gunsmoke thinned and cleared, torn away by the castle's undying wind.

The groogleman lay splayed out on the floor, with a huge red stain all over the white hide of its torso. Uncle Joshua reached out and grabbed the groogleman under the shoulders to pull it upright. "Help me!" he yelled at Dan.

Dan took the groogleman by the arm. The dead skin was cold and slimy to his touch and loose upon the bones beneath. He and Uncle Joshua carried the groogleman to Leezie's cell, and Uncle Joshua threw the body forward against the closed door.

Whatever spell had let the groogleman in and out still worked, and the door opened as the carcass touched it. The groogleman fell into the open doorway, and Dan saw that more blood ran from a hole in its wrinkled, gray-white back.

"Wait here," Uncle Joshua said, and entered the room. A moment later he reappeared carrying Leezie Johnson in his arms. Her eyes were closed, and she was trembling.

"Run," he said.

"But the groogleman is dead," said Dan.

"Run!"

A distant voice began to chant, echoing through the corridor, speaking words Dan couldn't understand. He ran, and Uncle Joshua ran with him, moving lightly in spite of Leezie's extra weight. Together they headed back the way they had come, through passages and rooms, while a keening sound echoed about them, as of inhuman things mourning, and the chanting voice never stopped.

Another groogleman appeared, coming

around a corner and shambling toward them. Uncle Joshua did not slow but instead swung Leezie to the floor and in the same movement unslung his rifle and slammed the butt of the weapon into the side of the groogleman's head. The groogleman fell.

"They can't see much of anything to either side," Uncle Joshua muttered to Dan, but he didn't explain how he knew. "You take Leezie on ahead—a hundred paces, no more. Wait for me there."

"What will you do?"

Uncle Joshua had his knife out. "A hunter wears the skin of his prey to get closer to the herd. Now go."

He put the knife to the groogleman's throat and pushed it up until the red blood came.

"Go!"

Dan helped Leezie to her feet and supported her as they walked on, while the voices in the air mourned and chanted, and wet sounds came from behind them where Uncle Joshua worked.

Before they had gone the hundred paces, Uncle Joshua joined them again. As he had promised, he was dressed in the skin of the groogleman— with nothing to show he wasn't real except his face poking out of the wrinkled white neck, and a dribble of blood running along the loathsome hide. He carried the skin of the groogleman's head, still dripping, in his hand.

"Now we go," Uncle Joshua said. They

walked on. Later he brought them to a halt again and said, "Don't look."

He moved out of sight behind them, and in a moment his breath began to hiss and bubble. Dan could guess what he had done: He'd pulled on the skin of the groogleman's head like a mask, enduring the blood and the foulness for the sake of the disguise. Dan and Leezie walked on, with Uncle Joshua shuffling clumsily behind them inside his stolen skin, until they came to the castle door.

Yet a third groogleman stood there, and the door was closed. Uncle Joshua called aloud, speaking a strange language in a harsh and hissing voice, and the groogleman turned away.

The door opened when Uncle Joshua touched it. Together, he and Dan and Leezie walked out of the grooglemen's castle into the night.

The three of them never went back to the Henchard farm. They buried the skin of the dead groogleman under a rock at the edge of the dead lands, then journeyed onward to the south, where there were towns and fishing villages all along the coast. Aunt Min had been right about one thing, at least: When Leezie grew a few years older, she married Uncle Joshua, and the two of them started their own clan.

Dan lived with them, and in time he brought home a wife from among the fisher folk. Later, when he was very old, he would sometimes tell children about his adventures in the castle of the grooglemen, and how Uncle Joshua won back Leezie Johnson after she had been stolen out of the living lands.

But one thing he never did tell, that he'd learned by looking back over his shoulder when he should have been helping Leezie walk away: When you take the skin off a groogleman, what you see isn't blood and meat and pale blue bone.

What you see looks as human as you or me.

5. (TS) Implementation. Biologic Sampling and Sterilization Command [BSSC] is hereby established under direction of SECEC. Existence of this command shall be close-hold to avoid alarming of civilian population. Full biologic safety is a priority. Assigned personnel shall wear full anticontamination suits, to include boots, gloves, gas masks, and self-contained breathing apparatus, at all times when in contact with nonapproved environments.

> —Annex K to ORDGEN 4B, TOP
> SECRET NOFORN WINTEL,
> distribution list Alfa only.

This is one of the first stories I ever wrote. It is also one of the silliest. I still love it.

FRIENDLY PERSUASION

Bruce Coville

Deep in the heart of an enchanted forest, beyond the Cinnamon Falls but not yet to the Grotto of the Red Mushroom, a tiny sprite named Sarinda dances on one broad leaf of a Dulcimer Plant. Her brief green toga flutters in the cool breeze blowing through the rich semidarkness of the afternoon shade. Her silken yellow hair flies gaily about her head.

Halfway through her dance she stops and stares straight ahead. A look of fear crosses her face. Lumbering through the trees is a huge Ba-Grumpus, most dreaded of all creatures in the forest. Deep grunts issue from the monster's fang-filled mouth. Its heavy orange body swings from side to side as it crashes over briers and tramples saplings. A terrible smell fills the air.

Suddenly the Ba-Grumpus spots Sarinda. Smiling wickedly, drooling, it makes straight for the leaf where the sprite was dancing but a moment before.

Sarinda narrows her eyes. Her look of fear is replaced by one of determination. "Too long have my people lived in fear of this monster," she whispers. "I will not flee from this bully again." And so she stands, a tiny golden arrow rising from the broad green plain of the leaf.

"Ooogly yummers," grunts the Ba-Grumpus, drooling and licking his hairy lips at the sight of his favorite dinner. "Woodsprite. Good meal!"

Sarinda quivers a little but does not stretch her wings, does not try to escape. "You don't want to harm me," she replies in a sweet, clear voice.

"Shut up, dinner," snorts the Ba-Grumpus. It is not used to resistance.

"I'll not be quiet," says the sprite defiantly. "It would be wrong for you to eat me. I have a right to live, too."

"What should I eat?" growls the Ba-Grumpus. "Grass?" It wheezes with laughter, astonished at its own wit.

"Far better to eat grass than to harm one hair of a living creature!" cries Sarinda, drawing herself to her full two-inch height. "Each has a right to life and love, a right to grow and be. You cannot end my time for the mere sake of your appetite."

"Shut up, dinner. Me too hungry for philosophy."

"I shan't be quiet!" cries Sarinda, quivering now with righteous indignation. "You are ghastly

71

and cruel to spend your time devouring my brothers and sisters. It is neither right nor meet."

"Meat it is," slobbers the Ba-Grumpus. "Why not eat you? Ba-Grumpuses got to live, too."

"But not at our expense! You must reconsider. Think of it. What if some creature a hundred times your size were to come along and try to eat you? How would you like that?"

The Ba-Grumpus pauses and thinks, which takes considerable effort. "That be bad," it says at last, its voice sincere.

"And what if you had to live in constant fear of being devoured by such a creature. How would *that* be?"

"Horrible," admits the Ba-Grumpus, tears filling its huge green eyes.

"Then why inflict such a fate on we sprites? Be merciful, and do unto us as you would have done unto you. Open your heart to my pleas, listen to your own essential goodness. Spare me and my kin, and live in peace with us."

"Nice idea," replies the Ba-Grumpus. "Too bad me still hungry."

With that it opens its enormous mouth and swallows the sprite in a single bite. Spitting out bits of leaf it has accidentally taken in along with the sprite, the Ba-Grumpus continues through the forest, feeling slightly dismayed that a good dinner has been ruined by too much talk.

The Modoc Indians lived in the lands that are now Northern California and Oregon. Their stories, recorded less than a century ago, give us a look at an older, earlier time—a time when monsters and giants roamed the earth. Working from one of those tales, world-famous storyteller Laura Simms takes us back to the world of the ancestors.

KOKOLIMALAYAS, THE BONE MAN

retold from a Modoc myth
by Laura Simms

In the earliest times when the world was new, a Modoc boy named Nulwee lived alone with his old grandmother. Every summer when the berry bushes were ripe for picking, the old woman told him a tale that made him tremble. Placing a berry basket in the boy's hands, she would say, "The Bone Man drank the river dry and devoured all the people except you and me. When you are old enough to be a warrior, you will bring the waters back, and people will live here once again."

Nulwee was frightened of the story. He was

still too young to be a warrior, but he knew that one day he would grow up. He did not know how he could kill a monster and bring the waters back.

"Grandmother," he asked every year, "what did the Bone Man look like?"

Her raspy voice shook as she answered. "He was all bones. Dry, gray, and too ugly. He wore a necklace made of human bones. He was as tall as a mountain, and his footsteps shook the earth."

When she tapped the berry basket and pushed him toward the door, he knew he should not ask more questions. But one summer, as he stood up, he saw that he was as tall as the old woman, so he added boldly, "Is that the end of the story?"

"The story is not ended because Kokolimalayas the Bone Man is not dead. He is only sleeping."

"Grandmother, where does the Bone Man sleep?"

"I do not know where the monster sleeps. I only know that you must be careful. When you walk, sing the old songs I taught you when you were small. They will strengthen your heart and the earth. One day you will kill the Bone Man."

Nulwee walked outside quickly. He wanted to forget his grandmother's words. Instead of singing the old songs, he sang his childish name song louder and louder as he walked toward the bushes: "Nulwee, Nulwee, Nulwee."

Picking berries in the warm sunlight, he soon forgot her warning. He walked, singing his name and picking berries, until the basket was full.

He stopped suddenly. He had walked all the way to the muddy path that had once been a river. Then he remembered his grandmother's warning.

Trembling, he began to sing her songs.

A cold wind sent a shiver down his spine. In the distance he heard a rattling sound. The earth shook.

Nulwee held tight the basket of berries and ran all the way back to the house. He didn't tell his grandmother what he had heard. But, in his heart, he knew that he had awakened the Bone Man.

The next day he returned to the riverbed. Although he was afraid, he was drawn to the rattling sound. Picking berries all the way, singing the songs, he imagined the Bone Man walking across a village and breaking houses like twigs beneath his feet.

He wanted to run away, but his feet would not listen. Then he heard the sound again. The noise began like the clattering of animal hooves in the distance. It grew as loud as clicking sticks. It came close like the rattling of deer toe rattles and turtle shell shakers that he had heard when the people danced long ago. Then the cold wind blew and the earth shook.

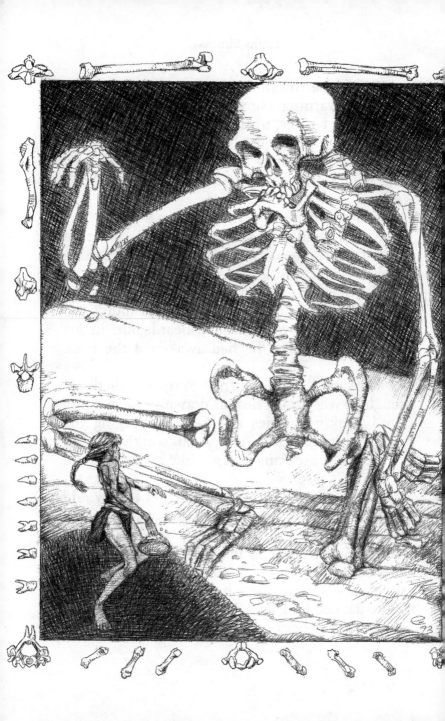

Nulwee's teeth chattered. His knees wobbled as he saw the monster rise up on the other side of the riverbed.

It grew, bone upon bone. He saw legs and back. He watched the long neck and round skull of the head rise up. He saw the mouth with no lips and bone teeth.

Kokolimalayas reached out with his hand of bone and grabbed the berries from the basket. He spoke, making a sound like wind racing through a hollow branch. "I'M HUNGRY!" Then he swayed and sang:

> *I am awake and I am hungry.*
> *I am the Bone Man.*
> *Sing your Song.*
> *Feed me and make me strong.*

When almost all the berries were gobbled, Nulwee ran back to his grandmother's house.

"What is wrong?" she asked.

Ashamed to have wakened the Bone Man, Nulwee answered, "The earth is too dry, Grandmother. There are very few berries."

The next day he gathered more berries, hoping that if he fed the Bone Man, the monster would not harm his grandmother.

As the monster ate, his bone necklace swayed. The birds stopped singing. He ordered,

Kokolimalayas, the Bone Man

"Nulwee, sing your grandmother's songs." The boy sang. The monster was growing bigger.

"Sing louder!" ordered the monster.

Trembling, Nulwee sang louder.

Nulwee did not have the courage to tell his grandmother about the Bone Man. But he saw that she was watching him carefully. Then one night she gave him a bundle wrapped in deerskin. Inside he found a painted bow and six arrows.

"These were made for you by your father. Now you are old enough to become a warrior. You must learn to shoot the arrows."

During the day the boy fed the monster. At night he practiced shooting the bow and arrow. He was exhausted. He knew that the monster was gaining strength and that as his strength grew, so did his hunger.

One day the monster emptied the basket in one gulp and said, "I am hungry. Soon I will eat you." As the monster laughed, Nulwee saw the berries drip down his chinbone like blood.

The boy stood fixed to the earth with fear. He could not speak.

Kokolimalayas stretched out his arms and said, "If you were a warrior, you would shoot me in the heart and kill me first. But you are just a weak child." Laughing, the monster turned and left. The earth shook. Trees in the distance bent from the force of the wind.

That night the old woman spoke as she pounded roots. "Nulwee, today I felt the earth shake."

Sorry that he had not spoken before, he moved closer to her. Her skin smelled of sweet grass and fire. He said softly, "Grandmother, I woke the Bone Man. He says that if I do not kill him, he will kill me."

The old woman closed her eyes and swayed back and forth, thinking deeply. "You must kill the Bone Man. I have told you that since you were a baby. That is what the old medicine man said when I took you to the mountains for safety the day you were born. The day that the Bone Man woke."

She was silent. Under her breath she began to sing a holy song. Nulwee was quiet.

He drank in the safety of her skin. He thought, I must destroy the Bone Man. I cannot let my grandmother be harmed. But I am afraid.

Finally Nulwee fell asleep. He dreamed, and in his dream the Bone Man was chasing him. Nulwee cried out, terrified, as if the dream were true. "Eat me. Do not harm my grandmother!"

His cries woke his grandmother. "You are very kind, Grandson," she said, placing her arm on his shoulder to comfort him. "I have dreamed, also. In my dream I spoke to the ancestors. They told me to tell you that Kokolimalayas is strong and dangerous. But he is not smart."

Nulwee listened with his ears, and with his heart.

"Brave Nulwee, to kill the Bone Man you must shoot him in the heart. He will try to trick you by showing you his chest. But his heart is not in his chest; it is in his little finger."

The old woman dressed Nulwee for battle. She painted red stripes across his face, his chest, and his thighs. She wove three feathers in his braids and blessed the bow and arrows.

"Grandmother, I am afraid," said Nulwee.

The old woman smiled. "A good warrior knows he is afraid and goes forward."

Nulwee set off for the riverbed. On the way he sang this hunting prayer:

My good bow and arrows,
You give me luck and strength.
I am going out to hunt now.
I will use you well.
Help me to have good luck hunting.
That's what I want you to do.

Then he filled the basket. When he reached the riverbed, he sang the holy songs.

The earth was silent. The monster rose up. He took the basket and swallowed all the berries. "Have you come to kill me, little warrior?" he asked, seeing Nulwee dressed for battle.

Pretending to be brave, the boy said, "Yes. I have come to shoot you in the heart."

Kokolimalayas spread his arms and bared his chest. Then, laughing, he lay down on the ground, arms open, and stared at the sky. "I will make it easy for you."

Nulwee knew that the monster could break his bones like twigs. He felt sick and wanted to run away.

The monster shouted, and trees bent on a distant mountain from the sound. "Hurry! If you do not kill me, I will eat you."

Nulwee stood as tall as he could. Slowly he lifted the bow and placed an arrow in the notch. His hands were shaking. Then he remembered the words of his grandmother: "Your father was a great warrior. Your mother was a medicine woman. You can call forth their strength to help you."

In that moment the boy became a warrior. He aimed his arrow at the monster's chest. Then, certain that the Bone Man was still looking up, he moved his arms and his eyes and aimed at the Bone Man's finger.

Nulwee let fly the arrow. It soared like a bird. It hit like a sharp stone.

The Bone Man screamed. "How did you find my heart?"

Suddenly Nulwee saw the heart fly from Bone Man's little finger. The boy dropped the bow and arrow and caught the heart in the basket. Without thinking, he began to run. Behind him he heard the Bone Man rising. Bone upon bone he was rising, to chase the boy. The whole earth was rumbling and quivering.

Nulwee ran as quickly as he could. The Bone Man seemed to gain speed, but without his heart, his body had no strength. Soon Kokolimalayas began to fall. His tumbling bones filled the riverbed.

The earth grew calm, and the birds began to sing. Nulwee lifted the heart and called out, "Kokolimalayas, you made a great noise when you were alive. Now you can make noise in the sky." He threw the heart into the sky and watched it whirl into the distance. It thundered loudly. Rain began to fall.

Nulwee sang a warrior's song:

> *When the boy becomes a warrior,*
> *The people all will live.*

Later that day Nulwee leaned against his grandmother's back and told her his story. She told him, then, the entire story of the day that she had saved him. "Your mother dreamed that you would one day destroy the Bone Man. So she wrapped you in a blanket and sent me into the mountains. Now that story is ended."

When Nulwee grew up, he became a great chief. The rains continued to fall and the river grew full, and people returned to the land. Whenever it thundered, the chief told the story of Kokolimalayas the Bone Man. He taught his children the songs of his grandmother, and they taught their children.

The land is abundant.
The river is full.
The people live safely.

It has been that way ever since.

The first short story I published was printed in an anthology called Dragons and Dreams, *edited by Jane Yolen. When the book arrived, I naturally turned to my own story, to see how it looked in print. Then I began to read the other stories. When I found this one I fell in love. After reading it to myself, I immediately called my son up to my room and read it to him. I have read it aloud many times since then, and it is still one of my favorites. I hope that you will like it, too.*

THE THING THAT GOES BURP IN THE NIGHT

Sharon Webb

He could hear it moving in the dark at the hollow of the stairs. He could hear it circling down there, snuffling, pausing, snuffling again. It was closer now. No more than a dozen steps away from his bed.

Shivering, John Thomas Caulfield clutched the thick quilt tighter and stared into the midnight room. He wanted it to go away. He wanted it to go away more than he had ever wanted anything in his whole life.

He never meant to call up the thing. Not really. He only did it to scare old Billy. Please, he thought. Make it go away. If it went away, he'd never ever be mean to his little brother again ever, no matter how rotten he was. "Oh, please," he whispered. "Make it go away."

Suddenly, a deathly quiet fell. John Thomas strained to hear. Then the sound came: a great intake of breath sucked through unspeakable nostrils. The thing was trying to get his scent. And when it did, it would know where to find him. . . .

It wasn't the Dutch-chocolate cake that made him do it. It wasn't even the sacred promise. It was because of the new baby. And why did his mom have to go and have an old girl, anyway?

John Thomas didn't have anything against girl babies. In general they were just as uninteresting as boy babies. He could take them or leave them, but what was hard to take was the way this one was messing up his life. It wasn't even in the house yet, and already things had changed.

It all started before supper. He had heard a thump in the kitchen and then a rattle-bang as the frying pan, whistle-clean from the cabinet, went sliding into the sink.

His mother stood there with her feet apart the way she'd had to stand since she'd got so big, and she was squeezing a package of pork chops. Squeezing hard. And her forehead was all squinched up.

"You okay, Mom?"

She caught her breath. Then she smiled. "I'm fine." But it was a funny smile, kind of lopsided and wobbly. The pork chops went plop onto the counter, and she spread her hands across her belly and cocked her head to one side as if she was listening to something.

He stood there, staring at her, not knowing what to do, when she said, "Pizza. I think I'll have your daddy bring home pizza for supper. Okay?"

Before he could answer, she said, "Call your daddy and tell him for me. I'm going to go lie down for a few minutes." She headed out, but on the way she stopped and clutched at the door-jamb. "Call him, John Thomas. And tell him to hurry."

He grabbed for the phone and dialed the drug-store. The baby, he thought. It had to be. The baby was getting ready to come. The other pharmacist answered and it was a couple of minutes until he heard his father's voice.

"Mom said to bring home pizza. She said to hurry."

"Pizza?" There was a pause. "I'll be right there."

* * *

John Thomas's father dropped the pizza box onto the kitchen counter and hurried to the bedroom. In a minute or so he came out carrying a suitcase. "It's time for Mom to take a little trip." He grinned a nervous grin at his sons. "Before you know it, you're going to have a new brother or sister, boys."

Let it be a brother, thought John Thomas. Let it please be a brother.

His mom came into the kitchen then. The same funny little smile flitted across her face when she saw him. "Kiss good-bye?"

He gave her a kiss. Not sure of what to say then, he followed it with a quick hug.

"You too, Billy," she prompted. She turned to her husband. "Will they be all right, alone here?" Little worry lines traced across her forehead as she looked at her youngest. "Billy's not even seven yet."

"Sure we will," said John Thomas. The idea of a babysitter at his age was ridiculous. After all, he was nearly a teenager, wasn't he?

"They'll be fine," said his father. He lowered his voice. "You'll have to be the man of the house for a while, John Thomas. You can do it, can't you?"

He nodded. "Sure."

"No hitting Billy, okay?"

He nodded again. "Sacred promise, Dad."

"And Billy, you're going to be a good guy tonight. I know you are. For Mom's sake."

John Thomas stared as his mother gasped and a startled look passed over her face. "I think we'd better go now," she said to her husband. "Right away."

His father snatched up the suitcase again. "Lock the door behind us, boys. I'll give you a call as soon as I have news."

When his parents had gone, the house seemed especially empty. John Thomas lifted the lid of the pizza box. Pepperoni, his favorite. But somehow he didn't feel very hungry. When Billy popped open two Cokes though, and they started in on the pizza, his appetite came back with a bang.

He ate so much, in fact, that he didn't have any room left for dessert.

John Thomas stared at the big wedge of Dutch-chocolate cake. "I'll have mine later," he said. Knowing that Billy would hog the biggest piece, he eyed the cake carefully and sliced it precisely down the middle.

Balancing his cake and a king-sized glass of milk on a plate, Billy went into the living room and switched on the TV.

The movie, which was about a haunted house, started with the warning, "Parental Guidance Recommended. This film may not be suitable for young children."

"I guess that means you, squirt," said John Thomas. "Go do your homework or something."

A look of outrage came over Billy's face. "Who says?"

"I said. I'm the man of the house tonight, and what I say, goes. And don't talk with your mouth full."

"Yeah? Well, you're full of it. And—"

And just then, the phone rang.

Billy beat John Thomas to the telephone. "A what? We got a what?"

John Thomas snatched the phone away in time to hear "—sister. A beautiful baby sister."

He scarcely heard the rest of it, only bits and pieces about Mom being fine, about Daddy having to meet Grandma at the airport, about his not getting home until the middle of the night. All he could think about was the baby and how it was going to ruin his life.

Why did it have to be a girl, anyway? If it was a boy, it would share a room with Billy. But an old girl got to have a room to herself. And that meant that he had to put up with Billy. Billy the Creep for a roommate. Whoopee. It was enough to make him want to throw up.

He went back into the living room, ready to lay down the law about "parental guidance." But Billy wasn't there.

John Thomas settled back to watch the movie when a loud crash came from overhead. His room. His stuff! He tore up the stairs and threw open the door. "You creep."

His model robot lay on its side on the floor.

The sheet metal was bent and the paint was scratched. He picked it up. The antenna was broken off at the base.

John Thomas raised furious eyes at Billy. "You stinking little creep. You broke it."

"I didn't mean to." Billy stared at the door and then back at John Thomas as if he was measuring the safety interval between them. "I was just moving it. It was on my side of the room."

"*Your* side?" yelled John Thomas. "I'm gonna kill you."

With a howl, Billy ran out of the room.

Fists doubled, John Thomas thundered down the stairs after him. It wasn't until he reached the bottom that he remembered his promise—his sacred promise to Dad. He stopped short then. "Curd face!" he hollered. He followed this with a string of four-letter words muttered under his breath so Billy wouldn't hear and tell.

Tonight he was the man of the house. And it stunk. But he was going to keep his promise if it killed him. He had promised not to get into a fight while Dad was gone. "You stinking slime!" he yelled. "Just you wait. Just you wait 'til tomorrow."

If Billy had been halfway decent after that, if he had been even a quarterway decent, then John Thomas would never have called up the monster.

John Thomas went back to his room. While

he was trying to fix his robot, he heard Billy down in the living room. Let him watch the old movie, he thought grimly. He hoped it scared the pants off him. He hoped it scared him so bad he'd have nightmares. It would serve him right.

He pressed on the robot with both thumbs and the bent sheet metal gave a pop. It was still dented though. He'd have to fill it with putty and paint it all over again.

The putty was all the way down in the basement. As he went down the stairs, eerie music came from the TV, and a woman's voice said, "There's something strange going on in this house. I know it, Richard."

The kitchen light was on. And there stood Billy, stuffing his face with Dutch chocolate.

"That's *my* piece of cake!" yelled John Thomas.

"You didn't want it."

"What do you mean I didn't want it?"

Billy gobbled another bite.

As John Thomas's hands balled into fists, two things came to him: his promise to his father—and the strange, scary music from the TV. Suddenly a brilliant idea struck him, and he drew a deep breath. "Put down the cake, creep, before I do something that'll make you sorry you were ever born."

"Oh yeah?" Billy's bottom lip was studded with crumbs.

"Yeah." Then, whirling, John Thomas ran into the living room to the bookcase. He scanned the shelves frantically. He needed a book. One that looked right. There. His fingers paused at the thick, dark medical book that belonged to his father. He pulled it out and read the gold lettering on the cover: *The Merck Manual, Thirteenth Edition.*

Waving the book slowly from side to side in time to the weird movie music, he walked back into the kitchen.

The cake paused halfway to Billy's mouth. He eyed his brother and then the door. "What do you think *you're* doing?" His voice was belligerent, but he looked like he was ready to run at the first sign of violence.

"In here is the wisdom of the ancients." John Thomas rolled his eyes toward *The Merck Manual.* "The magic spells of alchemists and wizards. And I know how to use them."

Billy snorted. "Sure."

"I can call up anything I want, Freak Face. A monster—anything."

"You say."

"Just you wait." John Thomas flung open the top drawer of his mother's kitchen desk and began to rummage inside. In the back, behind a stack of Green Stamps books and a crumpled package of petunia seeds, he found a tall candle a little flattened on one side. "First, the magic black candle."

"It's not black," said Billy. "It's purple. And you better not mess around in Mom's desk or I'll tell."

"The magic black candle," John Thomas repeated ominously. Another foray into the drawer produced a bent package of matches. He tore one off and scraped it. The match flared and touched the wick. He switched off the kitchen light. The candle flamed and made dark, flickering hollows beneath his eyes.

"I think"—John Thomas's voice dropped to a menacing whisper—"I think I'll call up a special monster. Just for you. A monster with yellow fangs as long as that"—He waggled his outstretched hand, and long, curved finger shadows slid across the wall—"And you can't hide from it. Anywhere. You know why?" He narrowed his eyes. "Because its nose is big as your whole head. It's got a big, green, gummy nose. And it can smell the chocolate on your breath and find you. Even in the dark. And when it does, it's gonna eat your face."

"You're full of it," said Billy. But his voice quavered just a little bit.

"Yeah?" John Thomas thrust the candle into a jelly glass and thumbed open the book to the red-tabbed index marked "Rx." The thin paper crackled as he turned the pages deliberately. Then he stopped, fixed Billy with a long stare, and tapped a section with his index finger. "Here it is." Raising his eyes to the ceiling, he said in a loud voice: "Monster-r-r. Hear me, Monster-r-r. Rise from the depths and get old Billy."

Billy's gaze slid uneasily toward the basement door.

"Cascara Sagrada"—John Thomas's voice deepened as he read—"Magaldrate. Oxethazaine in Alumina. Psyllium. Hydrophilic. Mucilloid."

A long wavering scream came from the TV.

Billy's eyes, wide now, glided back toward the flickering candle.

"Magnesia Magma," boomed John Thomas. "Kaolin."

Billy's teeth caught his lower lip.

"Pectin," John Thomas commanded. "Pectin . . . pectin . . ." he flung out his arms and bellowed, "Pectin-n-n-n. . . ."

A thick silence followed.

"It's coming now. It's gonna come when you're asleep. In the dark. . . ." John Thomas blew out the candle.

In the blackness that dropped like a thick curtain, he grinned at the little gasp that came from Billy's direction.

A scuffling sound.

The blue-white fluorescent light flashed on above the sink. Billy stood frozen, his hand on the light switch, his eyes staring wildly at the basement door. He blinked then, and looked down at the countertop and the wedge of Dutch chocolate. "I didn't want the old cake, anyway," he said, and slowly shoved the plate away.

"It's too late. There isn't any way to stop it now."

Billy's voice quavered. "Quit it, John Thomas."

"It's coming. It can smell the chocolate on your breath."

"Quit it. Quit." Then Billy was running out of the kitchen and up the stairs.

At the look on Billy's face, John Thomas felt a quick pang of guilt, but it passed in a moment and he reached for the uneaten cake. A minute later, he heard water running in the upstairs bathroom, and a little whishing sound.

Mouth full of Dutch chocolate, he grinned. Billy was brushing his teeth. Hard. As if his life depended on it.

Half wanting to watch the end of the ghost movie, half afraid to, John Thomas stared at the TV. He caught his breath as the music wailed into a wavering scream.

Then it was over. As the credits rolled, he got up and turned off the set. An eerie silence fell over the house.

Billy's probably asleep now, he thought. He hadn't heard a sound out of him for nearly an hour.

The kitchen was gloomy. The dim light over the stove accented the dark corners of the room. Looking for a snack, John Thomas opened the pantry and found a package of Oreos. The box was nearly empty; there were only two broken cookies left. Munching on them, he opened the basement door.

He had planned to go down and get the putty he needed to repair his robot, but when he switched on the light over the basement stairs, the single bulb hissed and went out.

A stale puff of basement air blew into his face. Like a breath, he thought. Suddenly, the dark stairway seemed to yawn like a giant throat. Whirling, he ran out of the kitchen and up to his room.

John Thomas pulled on his pajamas, jumped into bed, and turned off the light. The darkness closed in around him. He snuggled under the bedcovers and shut his eyes. Then he heard it: a low sigh moaning up the stairs. A distant sigh that seemed to come from the basement—that seemed to rise from the depths.

There's nothing there, he told himself. Nothing. Nothing at all.

Silence.

Then he heard it again: a sound that might have been the wind—might have been, except for the faint snuffling sound like air sucked into giant, gummy nostrils.

It's not anything, he thought. He could hear it

moving, coming up the basement stairs. The door! The basement door. He had left it open.

You can't hide from it. Anywhere.

The snuffling was louder. John Thomas could hear it over the pounding of his heart. A faint skittering sound came then: a sound that something large and scaly would make if it tried to move across a vinyl floor. It was in the kitchen now. It had to be.

A pause and then a low snort as if green and gummy nostrils flared and sniffed the air.

It can smell the chocolate on your breath.

The Oreos! He had eaten Oreos, and before that Dutch chocolate—and he hadn't even brushed his teeth.

It's coming for you in the dark. It's going to eat your face.

Oh, please. Make it go away.

Eyes squeezed shut, he huddled in the bed and tried not to breathe. Then he heard a sharp hiss and something skittered across the nape of his neck.

John Thomas thought his heart would stop.

The hiss came again. And the touch on his neck became the prod and poke of a finger. "Wake up," came a whisper. "I heard something."

It was Billy. Whirling toward him in a tangle of bedclothes, John Thomas felt his heart start again and bang against his chest. "What? Where?" But he knew the answer. Billy had heard it too. The monster was coming for both of them.

"I'm scared." Billy's whisper shivered into his ear. "It's gonna get me."

John Thomas tried to say, "No it's not," but his voice died in his throat. The skittering sound from the kitchen changed to a low thump-bump. The stairs! It was coming up the stairs!

"It's gonna eat my face."

John Thomas could smell the toothpaste on Billy's breath and underneath the faint sweet smell of . . . chocolate. He leaped out of bed. "It can smell us," he whispered. "We've got to hide." But where? Where? He stared wildly around in the dark. "Under the bed." But even as he said it, he knew that the monster would find them there. It would spread its awful green and gummy nostrils and sniff and know where they were hiding.

"What's it want?"

Us, he thought. It wants us. "We smell like chocolate. And that's what it eats."

A faint sniff—but this time it came from Billy. Then he said, "What if we give it my Oreos?"

"Oreos?" John Thomas's whisper was sharp. "You got Oreos?"

"In my room. I was saving them."

John Thomas thought fast—faster, maybe, than he had ever thought in his life. Billy's room was across the hall, closer to the stairs. Could they make it? But what choice did they have?

Another thump came.

Another.

"Hurry. . . . And be quiet." John Thomas grabbed Billy's hand, and they were running, bumping in the dark, scurrying across the hall into Billy's room.

The door shut behind them with a little thud. But there was no lock. No lock. No way to keep it out.

The moon made dark shadows stretch across the room. Billy reached for the light switch, but John Thomas grabbed his hand in time. "No, don't!"

Another thump, muffled by the closed door.

"The Oreos. Quick!"

Billy reached under his pillow and brought out a baggie stuffed with the cookies.

John Thomas fumbled inside and pulled out an Oreo. Catching his breath, he moved toward the door and opened it—just a crack. The hall was black and spooky. He strained to listen.

Another thump.

It was near the top of the stairs now. Another step and it would be in the hall.

Clutching the bag of cookies, John Thomas summoned all his courage and ran into the hall to the head of the stairs.

Another thump.

It had to work. Had to work. Had to. He flung the cookie down the stairs and darted back into Billy's room.

Door open just a crack, the boys pressed close together and listened.

A low snuffling groan . . .

Thump-bump.

Thump-bump.

Not daring to move, they clung together in the dark.

Thump-bump.

It was going down the stairs.

Thump-bump.

It *was*. . . .

And then a faint but unmistakable *crunching* sound came from the bottom of the stairs.

"It's got the Oreo," Billy whispered. "Give it another one. Quick. Before it comes back."

They scurried into the hall. Just as the crunching stopped, John Thomas pitched another cookie down the stairs.

The Oreo landed on the floor and slid across the vinyl.

Thump-bump.

A slithering, scraping sound . . .

Crunch.

"Come on. We've got to follow it." Heart racing in his chest, John Thomas crept down the stairs toward the faint blue fluorescent glow coming from the kitchen. Not daring to show his face, he stretched out his arm and pitched another cookie straight toward the basement door.

The boys pressed hard against the wall of the stairway. The baggie felt clammy in John Thomas's hand. There were just two cookies left. Just two.

Scrape-thud.

Scrape-thud.

Scrape-thud.

It was by the basement door now, he was sure.

Crunch.

John Thomas grabbed for a cookie. The basement stairs. He had to throw it down the basement stairs. Then he could shut the door. And lock it. He reached out—and gasped in horror. The cookie popped out of his hand, fell no more than three feet away, and rolled behind the breakfast bar.

Scrape-thud.

Oh no.

Scrape-thud.

It was coming back!

Scrape-thud.

C-R-U-N-C-H.

Just one cookie left. Just one. Just one.

John Thomas darted into the kitchen and flung the last Oreo down the basement stairs.

Then as something—something awful—scuffled behind the breakfast bar, he scurried back to the darkness of the stairs.

Silence.

Thick, awful silence.

And then a dreadful, blood-curdling, snuffling snort.

Scrape-thud.

Scrape-thud.

Ka-bump, ka-bump, ka-bump.

It was going away, down the basement stairs. It was. It was.

Crunch.

John Thomas raced toward the awful basement stairs, grabbed the doorknob, and slammed. The door clicked shut. He scrabbled with the catch; he heard it lock.

"Is it gone?" came Billy's whisper.

John Thomas stared at the basement door.

A faint ka-bump.

Ka-bump, ka-bump.

He shook his head. "It's still there."

"Maybe it can flatten out," said Billy in a low voice. "Maybe it can come under the door."

And the cookies were gone.

"Can it, John Thomas?" Billy began to cry. "What are we gonna do?"

Chocolate, thought John Thomas. It was chocolate the monster was after—and boys who smelled like chocolate. "We've got to get rid of the smell." He flung open the pantry cabinet and stared inside. Then he knew what to do. He grabbed down a can, and then another. "A spoon. Get one quick."

Ka-bump, ka-bump.

With hands that shook, he grabbed the can opener, cranked it, and thrust the open can toward Billy. "Eat it quick." Then he was opening the second can and grabbing a spoon.

"Yuck! It's spinach!"

"Shut up and eat." With frantic haste, John Thomas dug his spoon into the second can and gobbled. His was beets.

"Uck."

"Eat or you die," said John Thomas with his mouth full.

Ka-bump.

B-U-R-P. . . .

And Billy ate. He ate a half a can of spinach in two bites and the other half in two more. And John Thomas gobbled a can of beets in no time flat.

And they were cold, and nasty, and altogether disgusting. But he didn't care.

They left the empty cans and dirty spoons right there on the countertop and ran upstairs. And they jumped into John Thomas's bed—both of them did—and huddled together.

"Are we okay now?" asked Billy—and his breath was a reassuring spinachy breath.

"I think so," said John Thomas. But then he heard a sound. He heard a scrabbling click and then a metal sound like a lock turning. His heart jumped up in his throat. Then he heard—footsteps.

And it was Daddy. Daddy coming home.

"I think we're okay now," John Thomas said.

And Billy yawned because it was so late and said, "Do you think we can ever eat chocolate again, John Thomas?"

"Maybe," he said, "and maybe not." He snuggled down deep into the covers next to his brother. And the last thing he thought before he went to sleep was: It isn't so bad, really, having to share a room with old Billy.

There are worse things.

Even monsters have their troubles. . . .

PERSONALITY PROBLEM

Joe R. Lansdale

Yeah, I know, Doc, I look terrible and don't smell any better. But you would, too, if you stayed on the go like I do, had a peg sticking out of either side of your neck and this crazy scar across the forehead. You'd think they might have told me to use cocoa butter on the place after they took the stitches out, but naw, no way. They didn't care if I had a face like a train track. No meat off *their* nose.

And how about this getup? Nice, huh? Early wino or late drug addict. You ought to walk down the street wearing this mess, you really get the stares. Coat's too small, pants too short. And these boots, now, they get the blue ribbon. You know, I'm only six five, but with these on I'm nearly seven feet! That's some heels.

But listen, how can I do any better? I can't even afford to buy myself a tie at the Goodwill, let

alone get myself a new suit of clothes. And have you ever tried to fit someone my size? This shoulder is higher than the other one. The arms don't quite match, and . . . well, you see the problem. I tell you, Doc, it's no bed of roses.

Worst part of it is how people are always running from me, and throwing things, and trying to set me on fire. Oh, that's the classic one. I mean, I've been frozen for a while, covered in mud, you name it, but the old favorite is the torch. And I *hate* fire. Which reminds me, think you could refrain from smoking, Doc? Sort of makes me nervous.

See, I was saying about the fire. They've trapped me in windmills, castles, and labs. All sorts of places. Some guy out there in the crowd always gets the wise idea about the fire, and there we go again, Barbecue City. Let me tell you, Doc, I've been lucky. Spell that L-U-C-K-Y. We're talking a big lucky here. I mean, that's one reason I look as bad as I do. These holes in this already ragged suit . . . Yeah, that's right, bend over. Right there, see? This patch of hide was burned right off my head, Doc, and it didn't feel like no sunburn either. I mean it hurt.

And I've got no childhood. Just a big dumb boy all my life. No dates. No friends. Nothing. Just this personality complex, and this feeling that everybody hates me on sight.

If I ever get my hands on Victor, or Igor, oh

boy, gonna have to snap 'em, Doc. And I can do it, believe me. That's where they crapped in the mess kit, Doc. They made me strong. Real strong.

Give me a dime. Yeah, thanks.

Now watch this. Between thumb and finger. *Uhhhh.* How about that? Flat as a pancake.

Yeah, you're right. I'm getting a little excited. I'll lay back and take it easy.

Say, do you smell smoke?

Doc?

Doc?

Doc, damn you, put out that fire! Not you, too? Hey, I'm not a bad guy, really. Come back here, Doc! Don't leave me in here. Don't lock that door!

I thought of this story one afternoon while walking in the woods with some friends. When we got back from the walk, I excused myself, went upstairs, and wrote it down. I have never written a story that fast before or since. (Hey, I figure if you write for twenty years, you ought to get a break at least once!)

DUFFY'S JACKET

Bruce Coville

If my cousin Duffy had the brains of a turnip it never would have happened. But as far as I'm concerned, Duffy makes a turnip look bright. My mother disagrees. According to her, Duffy is actually very bright. She claims the reason he's so scatterbrained is that he's too busy being brilliant inside his own head to remember everyday things. Maybe. But hanging around with Duffy means you spend a lot of time saying, "Your glasses, Duffy," or "Your coat, Duffy," or—well, you get the idea: a lot of three-word sentences that start with "Your," end with "Duffy," and have words like "book," "radio," "wallet," or whatever it is he's just put down and left behind, stuck in the middle.

Me, I think turnips are brighter.

But since Duffy's my cousin, and since my mother and her sister are both single parents, we tend to do a lot of things together—like camping, which is how we got into the mess I want to tell you about.

Personally, I thought camping was a big mistake. But since Mom and Aunt Elise are raising the three of us—me, Duffy, and my little sister, Marie—on their own, they're convinced they have to do man-stuff with us every once in a while. I think they read some kind of book that said me and Duffy would come out weird if they don't. You can take him camping all you want. It ain't gonna make Duffy normal.

Anyway, the fact that our mothers were getting wound up to do something fatherly, combined with the fact that Aunt Elise's boss had a friend who had a friend who said we could use his cabin, added up to the five of us bouncing along this horrible dirt road late one Friday in October.

It was late because we had lost an hour going back to get Duffy's suitcase. I suppose it wasn't actually Duffy's fault. No one remembered to say, "Your suitcase, Duffy," so he couldn't really have been expected to remember it.

"Oh, Elise," cried my mother, as we got

deeper into the woods. "Aren't the leaves beautiful?"

That's why it doesn't make sense for them to try to do man-stuff with us. If it had been our fathers, they would have been drinking beer and burping and maybe telling dirty stories, instead of talking about the leaves. So why try to fake it?

Anyway, we get to this cabin, which is about eighteen million miles from nowhere, and to my surprise, it's not a cabin at all. It's a house. A big house.

"Oh, my," said my mother as we pulled into the driveway.

"Isn't it great?" chirped Aunt Elise. "It's almost a hundred years old, back from the time when they used to build big hunting lodges up here. It's the only one in the area still standing. Horace said he hasn't been able to get up here in some time. That's why he was glad to let us use it. He said it would be good to have someone go in and air the place out."

Leave it to Aunt Elise. This place didn't need airing out—it needed fumigating. I never saw so many spider webs in my life. From the sounds we heard coming from the walls, the mice seemed to have made it a population center. We found a total of two working light bulbs: one in the kitchen, and one in the dining room, which was paneled with dark wood and had a big stone fireplace at one end.

"Oh, my," said my mother again.

Duffy, who's allergic to about fifteen different things, started to sneeze.

"Isn't it charming?" said Aunt Elise hopefully.

No one answered her.

Four hours later we had managed to get three bedrooms clean enough to sleep in without getting the heebie-jeebies—one for Mom and Aunt Elise, one for Marie, and one for me and Duffy. After a supper of beans and franks we hit the hay, which I think is what our mattresses were stuffed with. As I was drifting off, which took about thirty seconds, it occurred to me that four hours of housework wasn't all that much of a man-thing, something it might be useful to remember the next time Mom got one of these plans into her head.

Things looked better in the morning when we went outside and found a stream where we could go wading. ("Your sneakers, Duffy.")

Later we went back and started poking around the house, which really was enormous.

That was when things started getting a little spooky. In the room next to ours I found a message scrawled on the wall. BEWARE THE SENTINEL, it said in big black letters.

When I showed Mom and Aunt Elise, they said it was just a joke, and got mad at me for frightening Marie.

Marie wasn't the only one who was frightened.

We decided to go out for another walk. ("Your lunch, Duffy.") We went deep into the woods, following a faint trail that kept threatening to disappear, but never actually faded away altogether. It was a hot day, even in the deep woods, and after a while we decided to take off our coats.

When we got back and Duffy didn't have his jacket, did they get mad at him? My mother actually had the nerve to say, "Why didn't you remind him? You know he forgets things like that."

What do I look like, a walking memo pad?

Anyway, I had other things on my mind—like the fact that I was convinced someone had been following us out of the woods.

I tried to tell my mother about it, but first she said I was being ridiculous, and then she accused me of trying to sabotage the trip.

So I shut up. But I was pretty nervous, especially when Mom and Aunt Elise announced that they were going into town—which was twenty miles away—to pick up some supplies (like light bulbs).

"You kids will be fine on your own," said Mom cheerfully. "You can make popcorn and play Monopoly. And there's enough soda here for you to make yourselves sick on."

And with that they were gone.

It got dark.

We played Monopoly.

They didn't come back. That didn't surprise me. Since Duffy and I were both fifteen they felt it was okay to leave us on our own, and Mom had warned us they might decide to have dinner at the little inn we had seen on the way up.

But I would have been happier if they had been there.

Especially when something started scratching on the door.

"What was that?" said Marie.

"What was what?" asked Duffy.

"That!" she said, and this time I heard it too. My stomach rolled over and the skin at the back of my neck started to prickle.

"Maybe it's the Sentinel!" I hissed.

"Andrew!" yelled Marie. "Mom told you not to say that."

"She said not to try to scare you," I said. "I'm not. *I'm scared!* I told you I heard something following us in the woods today."

Scratch, scratch.

"But you said it stopped," said Duffy. "So how would it know where we are now?"

"I don't know. I don't know what it is. Maybe it tracked us, like a bloodhound."

Scratch, scratch.

"Don't bloodhounds have to have something to give them a scent?" asked Marie. "Like a piece of clothing, or—"

We both looked at Duffy.

"Your jacket, Duffy!"

Duffy turned white.

"That's silly," he said after a moment.

"There's something at the door," I said frantically. "Maybe it's been lurking around all day, waiting for our mothers to leave. Maybe it's been waiting for years for someone to come back here."

Scratch, scratch.

"I don't believe it," said Duffy. "It's just the wind moving a branch. I'll prove it."

He got up and headed for the door. But he didn't open it. Instead he peeked through the window next to it. When he turned back, his eyes looked as big as the hard-boiled eggs we had eaten for supper.

"There's something out there!" he hissed. *"Something big!"*

"I told you," I cried. "Oh, I knew there was something there."

"Andrew, are you doing this just to scare me?" said Marie. "Because if you are—"

Scratch, scratch.

"Come on," I said, grabbing her by the hand. "Let's get out of here."

I started to lead her up the stairs.

"Not there!" said Duffy. "If we go up there we'll be trapped."

"You're right," I said. "Let's go out the back way!"

The thought of going outside scared the daylights out of me. But at least out there we would have somewhere to run. Inside—well, who knew what might happen if the thing found us inside.

We went into the kitchen.

I heard the front door open.

"Let's get out of here!" I hissed.

We scooted out the back door. "What now?" I wondered, looking around frantically.

"The barn," whispered Duffy. "We can hide in the barn."

"Good idea," I said. Holding Marie by the hand, I led the way to the barn. But the door was held shut by a huge padlock.

The wind was blowing harder, but not hard enough to hide the sound of the back door of the house opening, and then slamming shut.

"Quick!" I whispered. "It knows we're out here. Let's sneak around front. It will never expect us to go back into the house."

Duffy and Marie followed me as I led them behind a hedge. I caught a glimpse of something heading toward the barn and swallowed nervously. It was big. Very big.

"I'm scared," whispered Marie.

"Shhhh!" I hissed. "We can't let it know where we are."

We slipped through the front door. We locked

it, just like people always do in the movies, though what good that would do I couldn't figure, since if something really wanted to get at us it would just break the window and come in.

"Upstairs," I whispered.

We tiptoed up the stairs. Once we were in our bedroom, I thought we were safe. Crawling over the floor, I raised my head just enough to peek out the window. My heart almost stopped. Standing in the moonlight was an enormous, manlike creature. It had a scrap of cloth in its hands. It was looking around—looking for us. I saw it lift its head and sniff the wind. To my horror, it started back toward the house.

"It's coming back!" I yelped, more frightened than ever.

"How does it know where we are?" said Marie.

But I knew how. It had Duffy's jacket. It was tracking us down, like some giant bloodhound.

We huddled together in the middle of the room, trying to think of what to do.

A minute later we heard it.

Scratch, scratch.

None of us moved.

Scratch, scratch.

We stopped breathing, then jumped up in alarm at a terrible crashing sound.

The door was down.

Duffy's Jacket

We hunched back against the wall as heavy footsteps came clomping up the stairs.

I wondered what our mothers would think when they got back. Would they find our bodies? Or would there be nothing left of us at all?

Thump. Thump. Thump.

It was getting closer.

Thump. Thump. Thump.

It was outside the door.

Knock, knock.

"Don't answer!" hissed Duffy.

Like I said, he doesn't have the brains of a turnip.

It didn't matter. The door wasn't locked. It came swinging open. In the shaft of light I saw a huge figure. The Sentinel of the Woods! It had to be. I thought I was going to die.

The figure stepped into the room. Its head nearly touched the ceiling.

Marie squeezed against my side tighter than a tick in a dog's ear.

The huge creature sniffed the air. It turned in our direction. Its eyes seemed to glow. Moonlight glittered on its fangs.

Slowly the Sentinel raised its arm. I could see Duffy's jacket dangling from its fingertips.

And then it spoke.

"You forgot your jacket, stupid."

It threw the jacket at Duffy, turned around, and stomped down the stairs.

Which is why, I suppose, no one has had to remind Duffy to remember his jacket, or his glasses, or his math book, for at least a year now.

After all, when you leave stuff lying around, you never can be sure just who might bring it back.

What's waiting in the dark . . . ?

THE BOGEYMAN

Jack Prelutsky

In the desolate depths of a perilous place
the bogeyman lurks, with a snarl on his face.
Never dare, never dare to approach his dark lair
for he's waiting . . . just waiting . . . to get you.

He skulks in the shadows, relentless and wild
in his search for a tender, delectable child.
With his steely sharp claws and his slavering jaws
Oh, he's waiting . . . just waiting . . . to get you.

Many have entered his dreary domain
but not even one has been heard from again.
They no doubt made a feast for the butchering beast
and he's waiting . . . just waiting . . . to get you.

In that sulphurous, sunless and sinister place
he'll crumple your bones in his bogey embrace.
Never never go near if you hold your life dear,
for oh! . . . what he'll do . . . when he gets you!

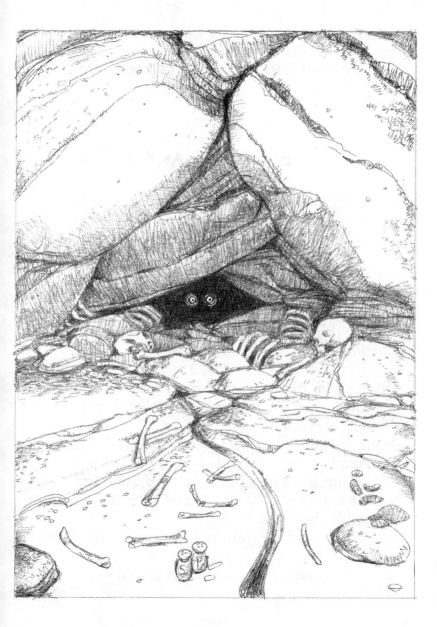

I met Patrick Bone while I was teaching a writing workshop in Colorado. Shortly afterward he sent me this short story, which gave me the shivers.

BLOODY MARY

Patrick Bone

"Go ahead, I dare you," I said to my stepsister, Juli. "Look into the mirror and say 'Bloody Mary' thirteen times. Of course, if you're a chicken . . ."

"I'm not a chicken," Juli responded. "I'm just not a child, like you are, Amanda."

She *was* two whole years older than I was. But she was also my very best friend in the world, even if we only saw each other every other weekend.

"I am not a child," I said. "I'm nine, and, I'm not afraid to say 'Bloody Mary' into the mirror. Here, I'll show you."

"Never mind." Juli took the mirror from my hand and held it in front of her face.

"You know the story," I reminded her.

"Of course I do," she answered. "I've known it lots longer than you. If you look into a mirror and say 'Bloody Mary' thirteen times, you'll turn into a monster."

"And the only way to reverse the spell is to say 'Bloody Mary' once in the mirror, in the *dark*," I added.

"Okay, silly," she said, "I'm ready. Prepare yourself for the most totally awesome monster you'll ever meet. You count.

"Bloody Mary."

"One."

"Bloody Mary."

"Two."

"Bloody Mary."

"Three."

I didn't believe in that dumb story any more than Juli did. But none of the kids I'd played with had ever tried it. Juli was the first, including me. Once I looked in the bathroom mirror and started saying "Bloody Mary." I stopped at twelve. I told myself it was stupid and I shouldn't bother about it. But I guess I was just a little scared.

"Bloody Mary."

"Thirteen!"

"There. It's done. Now, Amanda, see what a silly kids' story this is?"

Before I could answer, Juli got a mean look on her face. She bent over, low to the ground, and started to growl.

"Juli, are you okay?" I tried to say. But I just couldn't get the words out.

"BOO!" she yelled. "Fooled you, didn't I?" She laughed. "Ha, ha, Amanda believes in monsters, Amanda believes in monsters. . . ."

"Forget it," I said. "Let's play Barbies."

I knew that would get her. Even at eleven she still liked to play Barbies. I was her only Barbie playmate. She would have died if her classmates had seen her. But, somehow, with me, being her stepsister and all, it didn't seem to matter. We played till late.

Finally Dad said, "Time to go to bed."

Bed was the basement. In summer Juli and I slept down there because it was lots cooler. But the real reason was so my dad and Juli's mom couldn't hear us play and carry on all night long. The only problem was there were no lights down there. We had to lay out our sleeping bags before dark. When we went to bed, we would just play with the flashlight and talk or tell stories till we fell asleep. That night Juli told ghost stories. We stopped when the flashlight batteries went dead. But I wasn't afraid.

Not long after I fell asleep, I woke to a strange sound coming from right next to me. It was Juli. She was talking in her sleep or something. She sounded very uncomfortable.

"Juli," I asked, "are you okay?"

No answer.

"Juli?" Still no answer.

Then I heard her moan. I thought she was having trouble breathing.

"Juli?" I called out again.

"I'm not Juli," a voice answered. It didn't sound like Juli. It was low and growly and totally bad.

"Oh, come on," I said, "cut it out. You can't fool me twice." There was no response, just a scratching on the side of my sleeping bag.

"Stop it, Juli! You're scaring me!"

She stopped. Then, slowly, the scratching started again.

"That's enough," I said as I reached out to push her. That was a mistake. Instead of Juli's warm arm, I touched something furry and cold. I froze. "Juli, please stop this," I whispered.

"I'm not Juli," that terrible voice said again. I heard something reach toward me. By this time only the top of my head was sticking out of my sleeping bag. I felt long pointy things, like claws, run through my hair.

"Hungry," she growled.

"DADDY!" I screamed as loud as I could. I scrambled out of the sleeping bag. The only thing that saved me was that the *thing* also had to get out of her sleeping bag. She was much slower than I. I could hear her grunting like an old woman and scratching like a monster. By this time I was screaming, "DADDY!" louder than ever. But he didn't come . . . and she did.

"I'm so hungry," I heard her say. "I haven't

eaten in a hundred years! I'll gobble your nose and nibble on your ears."

Oh, gosh, I thought, *I'm going to be eaten by my stepsister! Even Cinderella didn't have to go through that!* "DADDY . . ."

The door at the top of the basement stairs opened.

"Amanda?" It was Dad! I felt so relieved. Now I would be saved!

"You kids settle down right now. Hear me?"

"Daddy!" I screamed. "Juli said 'Bloody Mary' thirteen times and turned into a monster with furry arms and claws, and now she's trying to eat me!"

"Sure," Dad yelled back. "Now get to sleep, or else!" The door slammed. I was alone again.

Dead meat, I thought. *Now what do I do?* The *thing* was still between me and the stairs. It was so dark that I couldn't see where she was. But that worked to my advantage. Every time she moved, I heard her and moved away. Trouble was, she stayed between me and the stairs so I couldn't run for it. It was only a matter of time before she caught me. I had to do something.

The mirror! I remembered. *To change the monster back to a human, you must get her to say "Bloody Mary" into the mirror in the dark.* But where was that mirror? And how would I find it with the monster trying to eat me?

I needed a plan to distract her long enough to feel on the floor for the mirror. *It's somewhere near my sleeping bag,* I remembered.

The closet! That's it! Trying not to make a sound, I felt along the wall for the closet. The monster moved. I stopped. *Is she reading my mind?* I could hear her breathing, low and raspy, like she was struggling to move. *At last!* I felt the closet door. Slowly, very slowly, I turned the door-knob until I felt the catch release. Then I swung the door open and yelled as loud as I could, "You can't catch me in here!" I slammed the door shut, hoping the monster would think I was trying to hide in the closet.

She started in my direction, and away from the sleeping bags. "You can't hide from me in there," she growled. "I'm so hungry. I would love a little girl right now. I haven't eaten in a hundred years. I'll gobble your nose and nibble on your ears. But don't worry, dearie. After a while you'll probably pass out and won't even know what I'm doing to you!"

I just about lost it then and there. But I knew I had to find the mirror. As the *thing* edged toward the closet, I crawled on the floor near the sleeping bag, feeling everywhere for the mirror. *There! No, that's a Barbie garage. It's here somewhere—I hope!*

I heard her at the closet. There was a sharp scratching sound on the door as if she was trying to find the knob, then the squeak of the doorknob turning slowly but not quietly. The door opened and I heard the monster shuffle. I could imagine her setting herself to catch me as I tried to flee. Then I heard the rustle of clothes and boxes.

"Where are you?" she whispered like a cat toying with a mouse. She got louder and screamed, "Tricked!" She slammed the door. "I'll get you for that! And I won't be nice this time. I will be fed. I haven't eaten in a hundred years. I'll gobble your nose and nibble on your ears. I'm coming for you, dearie."

She walked straight in my direction. I wanted to run for the stairs, but I knew I had to break the spell. I couldn't do it by running away. I had to face the monster and get her to talk into the mirror. After all, she *was* once my stepsister!

I still hadn't found the mirror. I began to grope wildly on the floor. *Barbie toys. If I never see another Barbie toy* . . . Suddenly she stopped directly in front of me. I held my breath. I could feel the wind her hairy arms made fanning the darkness right over my head, searching for me. *I won't give up without a fight,* I determined, as I silently searched for something to use as a weapon. *Ah, something hard and skinny. I can stab her with it. Oh, no, this can't be happening. Bloody Mary's about to attack me and I'm going to defend myself with . . . with Ken!*

In desperation I flung the doll at her—and

missed. It hit the wall behind her. She turned with a jerk. "You'll have to be quieter than that," she whispered, moving in the direction of the sound. As she shuffled away, I allowed myself to breathe again and continue my search.

Finally! I touched the I mirror. *Can I still do this? Well, it's now or never!*

Opening my mouth, I forced out the words, "I'm here."

"Ah, wait for me, dearie," she answered. I could hear her shuffle closer. She was still breathing heavily. Every step she took, she would say, "Hungry, sooo hungry." Suddenly she was standing right in front of me. I heard her moan.

But where, I wondered, *where should I hold the mirror?* Her breath directed me. *Ugh. Don't monsters know about toothbrushes?*

"Please," I begged. "Before you eat me, can you tell me your name?"

"Why, of course, dearie, you know me," she said with a cackle. "I'M BLOODY MARY."

There, I did it! It's over! She's changed!

"And I'm going to eat you, NOW!"

She hadn't changed.

I screamed as if it was the very last thing I was going to do on this earth and I wanted to make it last, "DAAAAAAAADDDDDDDDD-YYYYYYYYY!!!"

The basement door burst open. "Amanda, I

told you . . ." Before Dad finished his sentence, I was halfway up the stairs.

"Oh, Daddy, Daddy, please, please. Bloody Mary's going to eat me. Call the police, call the fire department, let's get out of here. I want my mommy!"

"Amanda, stop that NOW." Dad meant business. "You've had a bad dream. I'll just go down with you and tuck you back into bed."

"NO! No, please, Daddy, no. The monster, Juli, the monster, please!"

"Okay, okay," he reassured me. "I'll go down myself and show you everything is okay." Still crying, I stayed at the top of the stairs ready to go for help as soon as Dad screamed. But he didn't. Instead he called to me, "Amanda. Come down here. Now!"

Is he crazy? I thought. With every step down I imagined the monster raging up to eat me. Instead, at the bottom of the stairs Dad spotted his flashlight on the angelic face of my stepsister, Juli. She was sleeping like a baby in her sleeping bag. The change had finally taken effect.

"But, Dad—" I tried to explain. He cut me off.

"You've had a bad dream, honey," he assured me. "Now get back into your sleeping bag. We'll talk in the morning. And please, no more noise. We all need our sleep."

It was my turn to mean business. Wiping tears and snot with one hand, and pointing my finger up at Dad with the other, I declared, "Daddy, if you try to make me stay down here with Juli, I promise *nobody* in this house is going to get any sleep at all tonight." When I finally fell asleep, it was on the living room couch.

Dad woke me in the morning to get packed for the trip back to Mom's house. He didn't have to tell me twice. Going downstairs for my stuff wasn't nearly so scary as it had been in the dark. At the bottom I peeked around the stairwell. Juli was already awake. She was combing her long brown hair in *the* mirror. "Morning," she said. "Sleep okay? You tossed and turned all night. When I woke up, you were already upstairs. I hope you're all right."

I didn't answer. *Was it really just a dream after all?* I wondered.

Juli smiled. "I know! Let's play 'Bloody Mary.' You count. Bloody Mary," she said, looking into the mirror.

"Never!" I screamed, ripping the mirror out of her hand. While she sat there stunned, I walked over to the corner and threw it into the trash can. I paused, looking at the broken pieces of glass. That's when I heard the voice again, behind me.

"You shouldn't have done that, dearie," the voice rasped. "Thirteen years bad luck, you know. Starting now!"

I froze. I couldn't move if I had wanted to.

"Who—who's there?" I asked.

"Why, it's Bloody Mary! And I'm still very hungry. I haven't eaten in a hundred years. I'll gobble your nose and nibble on your ears. For breakfast!"

My fate was sealed. Slowly I turned to meet the monster about to eat me. There . . . stood my stepsister, Juli, with a great big grin on her face, holding her favorite stuffed toy, Tiger, with its big furry legs and long, sharp plastic claws.

"BOO!" she said. "Tricked you again."

I was so relieved I forgot to get mad. Instead I hugged her and said, "Oh, Juli, I love you." She must have thought I was crazy because all she did was stand there looking surprised.

"Five minutes!" Dad yelled. I ran to pack my clothes and Barbies and my jacket, which I saw over by the closet door. I crossed the room and was just about to bend over to pick up the jacket when something caught my eye.

"Scratches," I gasped. On the door, near the knob, were several long, deep scratches. Embedded under a splinter were tufts of short, dark, curly hair, and what looked to be a piece of broken . . . claw. *Is this real or another trick?* I wondered as I reached to touch the bits of hair.

"Something wrong?" Juli asked, standing immediately behind me. I turned with a jerk, hoping my back was big enough to cover the evidence.

"No. Just my stuff," I lied.

Juli smiled innocently. She pulled me to her in a great big tight hug. Then, she kissed me and whispered lovingly in my ear,

"See you in two weeks . . . *dearie!*"

There's more than one way to deal with a monster.

THE BEAST WITH
A THOUSAND TEETH

Terry Jones

A long time ago, in a land far away, the most terrible beast that ever lived roamed the countryside. It had four eyes, six legs and a thousand teeth. In the morning it would gobble up men as they went to work in the fields. In the afternoon it would break into lonely farms and eat up mothers and children as they sat down to lunch, and at night it would stalk the streets of the towns, looking for its supper.

In the biggest of all the towns, there lived a pastrycook and his wife, and they had a small son whose name was Sam. One morning, as Sam was helping his father to make pastries, he heard that the Mayor had offered a reward of ten bags of gold to anyone who could rid the city of the beast.

"Oh," said Sam, "wouldn't I just like to win those ten bags of gold!"

"Nonsense!" said his father. "Put those pastries in the oven."

That afternoon, they heard that the King himself had offered a reward of a hundred bags of gold to anyone who could rid the kingdom of the beast.

"Oooh! Wouldn't I just like to win those hundred bags of gold," said Sam.

"You're too small," said his father. "Now run along and take those cakes to the Palace before it gets dark."

So Sam set off for the Palace with a tray of cakes balanced on his head. But he was so busy thinking of the hundred bags of gold that he lost his way, and soon it began to grow dark.

"Oh dear!" said Sam. "The beast will be coming soon to look for his supper. I'd better hurry home."

So he turned and started to hurry home as fast as he could. But he was utterly and completely lost, and he didn't know which way to turn. Soon it grew very dark. The streets were deserted, and everyone was safe inside, and had bolted and barred their doors for fear of the beast.

Poor Sam ran up this street and down the next, but he couldn't find the way home. Then suddenly—in the distance—he heard a sound like thunder, and he knew that the beast with a thousand teeth was approaching the city!

Sam ran up to the nearest house, and started to bang on the door.

"Let me in!" he cried. "I'm out in the streets, and the beast is approaching the city! Listen!" And he could hear the sound of the beast getting nearer and nearer. The ground shook and the windows rattled in their frames. But the people inside said no—if they opened the door, the beast might get in and eat them too.

So poor Sam ran up to the next house, and banged as hard as he could on their door, but the people told him to go away.

Then he heard a roar, and he heard the beast coming down the street, and he ran as hard as he could. But no matter how hard he ran, he could hear the beast getting nearer . . . and nearer. . . . And he glanced over his shoulder—and there it was at the end of the street! Poor Sam in his fright dropped his tray, and hid under some steps. And the beast got nearer and nearer until it was right on top of him, and it bent down and its terrible jaws went SNACK! and it gobbled up the tray of cakes, and then it turned on Sam.

Sam plucked up all his courage and shouted as loud as he could: "Don't eat me, Beast! Wouldn't you rather have some more cakes?"

The beast stopped and looked at Sam, and then it looked back at the empty tray, and it said: "Well . . . they *were* very nice cakes . . . I liked the pink ones particularly. But there are no more left, so I'll just have to eat you. . . ." And it reached under the steps where poor Sam was hiding, and pulled him out in its great horny claws.

"Oh . . . p-p-please!" cried Sam. "If you don't eat me, I'll make you some more. I'll make you lots of good things, for I'm the son of the best pastrycook in the land."

"Will you make more of those pink ones?" asked the beast.

"Oh yes! I'll make you as many pink ones as you can eat!" cried Sam.

"Very well," said the beast, and put poor Sam in his pocket, and carried him home to his lair.

The beast lived in a dark and dismal cave. The floor was littered with the bones of the people it had eaten, and the stone walls were marked with lines, where the beast used to sharpen its teeth. But Sam got to work right away, and started to bake as many cakes as he could for the beast. And when he ran out of flour or eggs or anything else, the beast would run back into town to get them, although it never paid for anything.

Sam cooked and baked, and he made scones and éclairs and meringues and sponge cakes and shortbread and doughnuts. But the beast looked at them and said, "You haven't made any pink ones!"

"Just a minute!" said Sam, and he took all the

cakes and he covered every one of them in pink icing.

"There you are," said Sam, "they're *all* pink ones!"

"Great!" said the beast and ate the lot.

Well, the beast grew so fond of Sam's cakes that it shortly gave up eating people altogether, and it stayed at home in its cave eating and eating, and growing fatter and fatter. This went on for a whole year, until one morning Sam woke up to find the beast rolling around groaning and beating the floor of the cave. Of course you can guess what was the matter with it.

"Oh dear," said Sam, "I'm afraid it's all that pink icing that has given you toothache."

Well, the toothache got worse and worse and, because the beast had a thousand teeth, it was soon suffering from the worst toothache that any-one in the whole history of the world has ever suffered from. It lay on its side and held its head and roared in agony, until Sam began to feel quite sorry for it. The beast howled and howled with pain, until it could stand it no longer. "Please, Sam, help me!" it cried.

"Very well," said Sam. "Sit still and open your mouth."

So the beast sat very still and opened its mouth, while Sam got a pair of pliers and took out every single tooth in that beast's head.

Well, when the beast had lost all its thousand

teeth, it couldn't eat people anymore. So Sam took it home and went to the Mayor and claimed ten bags of gold as his reward. Then he went to the King and claimed the hundred bags of gold as his reward. Then he went back and lived with his father and mother once more, and the beast helped in the pastryshop, and took cakes to the Palace every day, and everyone forgot they had ever been afraid of the beast with a thousand teeth.

I have to tell you, this story is just plain sick. I don't suppose that's going to stop you from reading it, is it? All right, go ahead. But don't say I didn't warn you. . . .

TIMOR AND THE FURNACE TROLL

John Barnes

When Mrs. Docent announced that everyone would have to give a presentation on trolls next week, Timor was excited and scared at the same time. He knew most likely it would end up with the other elf-kids laughing at him again, because the magic for his presentations never came out right no matter how he tried. When the other kids gave reports on Martians in social studies class, or vampires in science class, they had no trouble making things appear and change. But when Timor tried, even the simplest things failed him. He had not managed to levitate anything in lab or to get the toy cowboys to talk about themselves in history class. And everyone had laughed at him.

Yet despite all that he was excited now, for

though he knew he had no knack for magic, he also knew he always had the best ideas for presentations and reports in the class. In fact, part of the reason they were always such flops was the difference between how big the idea was and how badly the magic turned out. So Timor's heart was already pounding, even before Mrs. Docent gave him the time pass for that week, the magic pass that let you go anywhere in the school for as long as you wanted and return to class the moment you left. There was only one given out each week, and it was only good three times; the student who got it was supposed to prepare a really special report.

On the other hand, Timor's joy was immediately squashed by Ferox, who loudly said, "Wonder what he'll waste that on."

Later, in lunch line, Timor found himself next to Gratia, a tall, thin elf-girl who was about the nearest thing that he had to a friend in the class. "How are you going to use the pass?" she asked.

Timor had been thinking about that all morning, right through geometry, geography, and geomancy.

"There's a lot you could do with it," Gratia went on. "You could spend a lot of time in the school museum, the library, or the art room. Or, you know, you could go to the AV room."

The Alchemical Virtuosity room was where

you went if you were a complete failure at magic. They were already sending Timor there twice a week.

"I'm going to see if I can use it to go to the furnace room," he said.

He knew it was a bold choice, but it was also about as good a hope as he had. In the furnace room there were cardboard boxes—some of the most powerful magic there was. Over in the Other Realm, where human beings lived, anything they put their imaginations into became magic, and all of that magic disappeared and came over here. Timor wasn't sure he'd ever even seen a cardboard box, because the ones that came over here were so shot full of magic that they were too powerful for elf-children to play with. But he knew they kept cardboard boxes in the furnace room, and if anything could work enough magic to overcome Timor's lack of talent, surely it would be a cardboard box.

In his imagination he could already see how impressed his classmates would be. Supposedly a cardboard box could become whatever you wanted it to. So he could make it be any of the great castles from the great sieges of the Troll War, or even the Dark Tower of Trollheim itself. In his mind, even now, he could taste the awe his classmates would feel, like warm sweet honey, as for once they admired Timor and liked him.

Gratia, who had been staring at him with her

mouth open, finally spoke. "That's such a great idea. And you're so brave. Are you really going to talk to him?"

To him! To whom! Timor thought. But he nodded anyway, not wanting to admit she knew something he didn't.

"I mean," Gratia said, "not many people even know there's a real troll in the furnace room. The only reason I know is that my mother is in KEKAFT, Keep Elf-Kids Away From Trolls, and they were trying to get rid of him because they thought it was too dangerous to have him here." Her voice dropped. "I hear he's twelve feet tall and covered with black greasy hair like what's on a dead mole. He has big old yellow tusks and keeps old bones to gnaw in there, and nobody knows what . . . or who . . . they come from." Her eyes were shining with excitement. "And you're going to talk to him. I can't believe how brave you are."

After lunch, because he knew if he delayed at all he would lose his nerve, Timor went up to Mrs. Docent's desk and told her he wanted to use his pass to go to the furnace room. She seemed a little startled, which didn't do his confidence much good. "Why, why, um, certainly," she said. "Not many people even know about Mr. Alfmordorsen. But I suppose you might learn a great deal. . . ."

She handed him the pass. Once he wished himself somewhere else, he could be there as long as he wanted, and when he came back here it would be the same time as when he left. Timor gripped it in his sweaty hand and wished . . . and nothing happened. The class roared with laughter.

Blushing, he realized it was not his fault—he had wished he was at home under his bed, which of course was off limits to the pass, since it only worked within the school. All the same, now all of them would have another story about Timor who couldn't do anything right. Still blushing, he wished himself into the furnace room.

It was red and flickering down here, for the furnace was a great open hearth. There were strange smells Timor had never smelled before— not terrible or evil, but very different.

Something moved in the dim red glow.

That had to be Mr. Alfmordorsen, rearing up from behind the pile of old books. He really was twelve feet tall, and might have been taller if he could have stood up. But his back was strangely bent so that his head seemed to stick right out of his huge chest. His teeth and jaws stuck out a long way in front of his face, and instead of the delicate, thin eyebrows of an elf, he had a great swatch of orange hair all the way across his forehead. There were patches of orange hair everywhere else on him, and a great shock of it, bound around a bone, stuck up from the top of his head.

Everywhere where there wasn't a tuft of orange hair, there was soft black fur, but it was nothing like a dead mole's—it looked soft and clean, like something you would want to run your hand over. And Mr. Alfmordorsen's two big tusks, which were sticking out of his lower jaw, though they looked sharp as razors and thick as Timor's wrists, were clean and white.

"Well, hello, and what can I do for you?" Mr. Alfmordorsen said.

Timor thought his teeth might chatter, but he screwed up his courage and said, "Please, sir, I'm here on a time pass, because I'm supposed to do a presentation on t-t-t-t—"

"On trolls?" Mr. Alfmordorsen's face broke into a warm grin. "Well, you came to the right place. What do you need to know?"

Timor had really only meant to ask, very politely, for a cardboard box, but now he could hardly disappoint Mr. Alfmordorsen. "Oh, um, everything, really," he said. "I don't know much, so I don't know what would be a good presentation."

All he knew about trolls, really, was that Elfland had had a war with Trollheim and won it. And he knew that trolls were only allowed in some parts of the city and couldn't go to the same schools, eat in the same places, or ride on streetcars with elves, and that at recess, whenever they played Elves and Trolls, the dumb and clumsy elf-kids, and the ones who had no friends, always had to be the trolls and get beaten up. He had always been picked for a troll himself.

"You want to know everything?" Mr. Alfmordorsen laughed, and it was a wonderful deep booming sound like happy thunder or a Christmas avalanche. "That's forty thousand years of history and poetry and painting, you know. Would you like to learn some of our music?"

Timor liked music, though he wasn't any good with the harp, lute, or lyre. "Sure."

"Well, I've got a few of my instruments here. Have you ever heard the trombone or the saxophone?"

Timor had not, but the moment he did he loved both instruments. And better still, when Mr. Alfmordorsen started to teach him, he picked them up very naturally, so that in very short order he and the troll were playing together, joyous music with more rhythm and laughter in it than Timor had ever heard before.

"It's so lovely," Timor said. He had now been down in the furnace room for two days, for elves eat little, and trolls eat rarely, and the only reason either of them sleeps is to have something to do at night. "Do any of these songs have words?"

"Of course," Mr. Alfmordorsen said. "Take the one that goes bump-ditty bump-ditty bump bump bump, for example. In Trollish, the words are:

*Kroncha alf, moncha alf, tchomp tchomp
    tchomp
Kooka alf shiska bab tchomp tchomp tchomp*

*Slya alf, dyza alf tchomp tchomp tchomp
Kozza alf ist fur tchomp tchomp tchomp.*

He didn't mention what the words meant, exactly, but it was a very funny and lively song, even if you didn't know, and shortly Timor had learned a dozen verses. "This will be perfect for my presentation," Timor said. He felt a little shy in asking, but did anyway. "Do you suppose I could borrow the trombone to show them, too?"

"Certainly! And if you like . . ." Mr. Alfmordorsen got up and moved his hairy bulk over to a dark pile in the corner. "Oh, here it is. I bet you've heard of the Troll War."

Timor gulped. "Oh, yes."

"Well, I was in that, you know. And here's my old field kit . . . the old sword, shield, and bow, and of course my eating utensils and sauce bottle." Even the eating utensils seemed big to Timor; the tines of the fork were as long as a full-grown elf's waist was thick. He hefted the fork in both hands. It was practically a weapon in itself, for someone Timor's size.

"Wow."

"You can show them the field kit, too, if you like."

"Oh, thank you!" In his mind's eye Timor could see the wonder on all his classmate's faces —even Ferox and especially Gratia. "What do the runes on the side of the sword say?" Timor asked.

"It's a Trollish word. *Alfschticker.* It's sort of like, oh, a trademark or a good-luck charm."

"Oh." The sword was so big Timor could barely lift it. A thought came to him, then. "How will I get your things back to you? The furnace room doesn't have a door."

"You have two trips left on your pass. Use one just before your report to come and get the field kit and trombone, and another just after to return them."

"I've had such a wonderful time here," Timor said. He was suddenly realizing how much he was going to miss Mr. Alfmordorsen.

"Are you all right?" The troll's big, dark eyes were kind.

"Well . . ." and then somehow Timor was pouring out all his troubles—how the other elf-children always picked on him, and how the magic never worked for his reports and presentations. "And I'm just afraid that . . . well, this is such great material, but I just know I'll flub the magic, and the other kids will laugh. . . ." He didn't mean to sniffle, but he did, and wiped his nose on his sleeve.

"Aw," Mr. Alfmordorsen said, sympathetically. "Don't worry about that. We have all kinds of magic down here. Would you like to see . . . the cardboard boxes?"

Timor had forgotten all about them, but now that he was seeing them—and with a friend—they were wonderful.

"A lot of human kids must think their mothers threw these boxes out," Mr. Alfmordorsen said, "but what happened is that they got full of imagination and all came here—spaceships, submarines, supercomputers, time machines, shrinking machines, transmogrifiers, all kinds of things. Now, just try working one and see if you don't have a little bit of magic. . . ."

They ended up spending another week, going to Mars and down into the Tonga Trench, traveling in time back to the Cretaceous and forward to watch the sun go out, making themselves small enough to visit their own bloodstreams and into hard silicon crystals to swim in the oceans of Saturn. It was more fun than Timor had ever had in his life, and the magic worked perfectly for him every time.

When at last they returned to the furnace room, Mr. Alfmordorsen showed him some trollish implements and let him try working magic—and not only did the magic work for Timor, but he even turned out to be good at it.

"See?" Mr. Alfmordorsen said. "You just had to find magic you had the knack for. Among us trolls, you might've made a wizard."

"I guess I should get back," Timor said, with more regret than ever. "I'll be getting back just an hour before a spelling test, and I'm sure by now I've forgotten all the spells."

"I've enjoyed your visit very much," Mr.

Alfmordorsen said. "Please come again and stay as long as you like, whenever you can get a pass."

"Isn't there any way you could visit me outside?" Timor asked. And then he remembered and felt stupid. Trolls weren't allowed in most of the city, and now that he thought of it, grown-up elves seemed to treat trolls very badly.

"They have a spell that keeps me locked in here," Mr. Alfmordorsen explained, very, very sadly. "If only I could get out of here, I could go wherever I wanted . . . but someone would have to take me out of here."

"Where would you go?" Timor asked.

"Even though we lost the war, there are still many free trolls living up in the hills of Troll-heim," Mr. Alfmordorsen said. "We aren't far from there. I would go join the Trollish Resistance, and then I could do trollish things all day long. The furnace room is warm and comfortable, but it's very lonely, and no place for a troll. Thank you so much for coming to visit."

Then they shook hands, and Timor wished himself back to class, the moment he had left it.

Everyone was still laughing at him. Then they gasped. "YOU STINK!" they exclaimed, in unison.

Mrs. Docent dragged him down the hall to the washroom. "Well, I'm sure you know all about trolls now!" she muttered as she scoured his skin raw. "You smell just like one."

For the rest of the day everyone called him "Troll-Boy" and made a big point of holding noses when he was near.

Timor couldn't smell the troll on his clothes, but everyone else said they could. He wished he could, because it might have been very comforting to smell something from the nice, warm furnace room. And he had never noticed before how much elf-soap stank of flowers and sunshine.

At recess Ferox invented a new game, called Roll the Troll. As far as Timor could figure out, the rules were that all the elf-boys took turns holding Timor down and hitting him.

As Timor, bruised and sore, followed his classmates back from recess, carefully keeping a distance so that the other elf-kids couldn't complain about his smell, Gratia dropped back to talk to him. "It will all be okay," she said sympathetically. "You just need to work harder at being more elfish."

"Thanks," he said.

"I'm sure you can if you try," she said, smiling sweetly. "Just think lots of elfish thoughts and really put an effort into it."

"Sure."

"I mean, it's not as if you don't want to be normal. I'm sure if you try hard enough, you'll get the hang of it. There's a good elf inside you."

"Thank you." He didn't feel better, somehow, but because Gratia was at least trying to be nice, Timor added, "You're very sweet."

"Of course. It's the elfish way to be. Ooops—
don't get too close. I don't want whatever's on
your clothes to rub off on me."

But in the days that followed, no matter how
hard he tried, he just could not seem to be elfish
enough. Every recess they played Roll the Troll,
until he felt as if he were just one big bruise. Every
day other kids sat farther away from him.

At home he worked hard on his presentation,
but somehow he couldn't get the elf magic to
work. Why was troll magic so much easier? He
asked Gratia, who was the only elf-kid who would
talk to him anymore, though she didn't like to
have the others see her doing it.

"Well, probably you can do troll magic because trolls are . . . you know. Stupid."

"They are?"

"Everyone knows that, dummy. My mom
says trolls are stupid." She tossed her long blond
hair to the side. "They're not much more than
animals. So naturally their magic must be really
easy. Whoops. Here come Amicitia and Adelpha.
Pretend I've been making fun of you, all right? Cry
or something."

At last the day for the presentation came. He
certainly wasn't looking forward to it anymore.
He took the pass and wished, and this time he had
no trouble at all wishing to be in the furnace
room.

Mr. Alfmordorsen already had the trombone
and the field kit packed and ready for him. "If you

like, we can spend a few days reviewing the trombone."

Just that little bit of kindness was enough to make Timor burst into tears.

Mr. Alfmordorsen picked him up and held him in his big, strong, hairy arms. The troll's fur was warm and soft and smelled good. Before he was quite aware he was doing it, he had told Mr. Alfmordorsen about all of it. "And now I have to go back to class, and no matter how good my presentation is, they're all sure to laugh, if they don't just scream and hold their noses just because I smell like a warm, friendly troll instead of like nasty sour old elf-soap." He started to cry again. "I wish I could be a troll like you!"

"But of course you can," Mr. Alfmordorsen said. "All you have to do is eat what a troll eats, and you'll become one."

"Really? What's that?"

Mr. Alfmordorsen told him. Timor was a little surprised, but then he thought about going back to the classroom and realized that in some ways this was the best part.

A few minutes later Timor, holding Mr. Alfmordorsen's hand so the troll could come with him, wished his way back to class. They popped into the classroom, and Timor could see that everyone had already gotten set to jeer and laugh, but that expression ran right off their faces when they saw the twelve-foot troll in front of them.

Then Mr. Alfmordorsen leaped forward and grabbed Mrs. Docent by her wrists and ankles, stretching her out like an accordion until you could hear all the bones in her spine pop, and bit the middle right out of her, gobbling down the pieces that remained in each hand as he moved to block the exit.

The other elf-children stared wide-eyed as Timor lowered the huge troll fork at them and forced them to back up against Mr. Alfmordorsen, who was gobbling them down like peanuts, with a great flurry of gulping and smacking, crunching bones, and elfish screams.

Ferox tried to get past Timor, and Timor ran the fork right through him; it was more fun than Timor had ever had before.

Gratia looked very, very frightened, and she said to Timor, "But I'm your friend, aren't I?"

"I won't feed you to Mr. Alfmordorsen," he said, shouting a little to be heard over the shrieks of Dulcitia, whom Mr. Alfmordorsen was lowering into his enormous jaws, nibbling her away from the feet up. "I think you're the sweetest elf-girl in the class, Gratia."

She was, too. And as he finished the last of his meal, Timor realized she had been right—there was now a good elf inside him. He wiped his mouth on a hank of blond hair, belched and stretched, and then crowed with happiness as he felt the black and orange hair breaking out all over his body, and the silly elf-clothes bursting and falling away as he outgrew them.

He had finished everything on his plate, and now, sure enough, he was growing up big and strong, just like Mr. Alfmordorsen.

ABOUT THE AUTHORS

JANE YOLEN has published well over a hundred books. Her work ranges from the slaphappy adventures of Commander Toad to such dark and serious stories as *The Devil's Arithmetic*, to the quietly beautiful *Owl Moon*, which was a Caldecott Award winner. She lives in a huge old farmhouse in western Massachusetts with her husband, computer scientist David Stemple.

MICHAEL MARKIEWICZ teaches history in a private school for troubled teens. He lives in rural Pennsylvania with his wife and "two totally spastic beagles," Penny and Nickel, which is not a reflection of their relative worth. This is his first published story.

DEBRA DOYLE and JAMES D. MACDONALD, a husband-and-wife writing team, have published nearly two dozen books under a variety of pseudonyms. Their most recent books under their own names include *Knight's Wyrd* (young adult fantasy), *Bad Blood* (young adult horror), and *The Price of the Stars* (adult science fiction). They live in New Hampshire with their four children.

LAURA SIMMS is one of America's best-known storytellers. A resident of New York City, she has traveled the world both as a performer and as a student of the stories of other cultures. Her books include *The Squeaky Door* and the forthcoming *Moon and Otter*. She frequently performs at New York City's Museum of Natural History.

SHARON WEBB has written for both children and adults. Her *Earthsong Trilogy*, written for young adults, features a future where we have achieved eternal life. She lives in Georgia.

JOE R. LANSDALE is a Texas-based horror writer known for his unique short stories. His books include *The Drive In*, *The Magic Wagon* and *Batman in: Terror on the High Skies*.

JACK PRELUTSKY is one of the most popular poets writing for children today. His books *New Kid on the Block* and *Something Big Has Been Here* were major bestsellers.

PATRICK BONE is a retired parole agent who has also been a ranch hand, minister, police officer, prison captain, and college teacher. He lives in Littleton, Colorado, where he writes, tells stories, illustrates, and teaches humanities courses at a community college. This is his first published story.

TERRY JONES was a member of the Monty Python comedy group and directed their film *Monty Python's Life of Brian*. He attended Oxford University and has a special interest in medieval history and literature. "The Beast with a Thousand Teeth" is from a collection of fairy tales that he originally wrote for his daughter.

JOHN BARNES is one of the most exciting writers to enter the science fiction field in recent years. His books include *Orbital Resonance* and *A Million Open Doors*. He recently completed his degree in theater history at the University of Pittsburgh. "Timor and the Furnace Troll" is his first story for younger readers.

JOHN PIERARD, illustrator, lives with his dogs in a dark house at the northernmost tip of Manhattan. He has illustrated several books in Bruce

Coville's *My Teacher Is an Alien* series. His pictures can also be found in the popular *My Babysitter Is a Vampire* series, in the *Time Machine* books, and in *Isaac Asimov's Science Fiction* magazine.

P.S. Still wondering where "Let the wild rumpus start" comes from? It was said by Max, the hero of Maurice Sendak's rollicking monster story Where the Wild Things Are.

BRUCE COVILLE was born and raised in a rural area of central New York, where he spent his youth dodging cows and chores, and reading things like *Famous Monsters of Filmland*. He lives in an old brick house in Syracuse with his wife, illustrator Katherine Coville, plus enough children and pets to keep life interesting. Though he has been a teacher, a toymaker, and a gravedigger, he prefers writing. His dozens of books for young readers include the best-selling *My Teacher Is an Alien* series, as well as the *Camp Haunted Hills* books, *Monster of the Year, Sarah's Unicorn*, and *Goblins in the Castle*.

CONTEST!
WRITE A SCARY STORY FOR BRUCE COVILLE

Bruce Coville wants to include a scary story written by one of you in his upcoming anthology *Bruce Coville's Book of Nightmares*! When asked what he thinks is scary, Bruce Coville responded, "I don't think gore is scary. It's too easy to toss around buckets of blood. I want stories that will make my spine tingle, not stories that will make my stomach turn; I want stories that will make the hair on the back of my neck (I don't have any hair on top of my head) stand up."

Read the contest rules below, then write a scary story and submit it to Bruce Coville. If your story wins, it will be published in *Bruce Coville's Book of Nightmares* and you will receive $100 and an opportunity to edit your story with Bruce Coville.

CONTEST RULES:

GRAND PRIZE: The winning entry will be published in *Bruce Coville's Book of Nightmares*, and the winner will receive $100 and an opportunity to edit his or her story with Bruce Coville.

RUNNERS-UP PRIZE: Fifty runners-up will receive a free copy of *Bruce Coville's Book of Nightmares.*

1. All entries must be submitted on 8 1/2" by 11" paper, typed and double spaced, with your name, address, telephone number, and date of birth at the top of the first page, and your name at the top of every other page. An entry should be at least 200 words, but should not exceed 2,000 words.

2. Contest is open to residents of the continental United States who are 14 years of age or younger. Contest is void where prohibited by law, and all federal, state, and local rules and regulations apply. Employees and immediate families of Scholastic Inc., General Licensing Company, Inc., and Bruce Coville, and their respective affiliates, retailers, distributors, and advertising, promotion, and production agencies are not eligible. No purchase is necessary to enter.

3. Mail entries to: BRUCE COVILLE CONTEST, c/o General Licensing Company, Inc., 24 West 25th Street, New York, New York 10010.

4. Entries must be postmarked no later than January 15, 1994. Scholastic Inc., General Licensing Company, Inc., and Bruce Coville are not responsible for late, misdirected, postage-due, or illegible entries. One entry per person. Entries will not be returned.

5. The winner will be determined by Bruce Coville, whose decisions are final. Entries will be judged based on the following criteria: creativity, originality, scariness, and quality of writing.

6. Winner will be notified by mail by April 15, 1994. Winner and winner's legal guardian may be required to sign and return an affidavit of eligibility within fourteen days of notification. The prize is the sole compensation for the winning entry. No substitution for the prize is permitted. Winner must assign all rights to the entry to Scholastic Inc. Taxes are the sole responsibility of the winner. The names and likenesses of winner and winner's legal guardian may be used for promotional purposes.

7 . In the event that there is an insufficient number of entries to meet Bruce Coville's minimum requirements, the sponsor reserves the right not to award the prize.

8. For the name of the winner, send a stamped, self-addressed envelope to BRUCE COVILLE CONTEST WINNER, c/o General Licensing Company, Inc., 24 West 25th Street, New York, New York 10010.